Elsa's mind shut down and she let herself just kiss. And be kissed.

The kiss was deep and long and magical, and as it finally ended, it was as much as she could do not to weep.

No! She made a Herculean effort to haul herself together. This was way past unprofessional. She could just about get herself struck off the medical register for this. But right now, she was having trouble thinking that it mattered, whether she was struck off or not.

This man's life was in Sydney. It could only ever be a casual fling with a guy who was bored.

"About that date…" he ventured, and she needed to shake her head, but all she could do was look up into his deep eyes, and sense went right out the window.

Then reality suddenly slammed back with a vengeance as the hospital speaker system crackled to life.

"Code blue. Nurses' station. Code blue."

Code blue!

What was happening with Marc was pure fantasy. This was the reality of her life.

She was out the door and she was gone.

Dear Reader,

Visiting the Buchan Caves, deep in the forests of southeastern Victoria, is an amazing experience. Narrow tunnels lead to deep underground chambers filled with breathtaking rock formations. My family towed me down to see and I was spellbound—and then they turned off the light. I wanted out, NOW.

When finally I surfaced—when I stopped shaking—my writerly mind was in overdrive. I couldn't wait to get home to hurl my hero underground and leave him trapped for my heroine to find. Because it was summer, I also wanted a gorgeous island coastal setting, and because it was Christmas, I threw in a Christmas feast with all the trimmings.

So here I give you *Mistletoe Kiss with the Heart Doctor*, a story that made me very happy to be safely celebrating Christmas aboveground.

Warm wishes to you all!

Marion

MISTLETOE KISS WITH THE HEART DOCTOR

MARION LENNOX

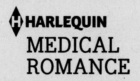

HARLEQUIN
MEDICAL
ROMANCE

HARLEQUIN®
MEDICAL
ROMANCE™

ISBN-13: 978-1-335-14982-4

Recycling programs
for this product may
not exist in your area.

Mistletoe Kiss with the Heart Doctor

Harlequin Enterprises ULC
22 Adelaide St. West, 40th Floor
Toronto, Ontario M5H 4E3, Canada
www.Harlequin.com

Printed in U.S.A.

Marion Lennox has written over one hundred romance novels and is published in over one hundred countries and thirty languages. Her international awards include the prestigious RITA® Award (twice!) and the *RT Book Reviews* Career Achievement Award for "a body of work which makes us laugh and teaches us about love." Marion adores her family, her kayak, her dog and lying on the beach with a book someone else has written. Heaven!

Books by Marion Lennox

Harlequin Medical Romance

Bondi Bay Heroes
Finding His Wife, Finding a Son

Falling for Her Wounded Hero
Reunited with Her Surgeon Prince
The Baby They Longed For
Second Chance with Her Island Doc
Rescued by the Single Dad Doc
Pregnant Midwife on His Doorstep

Harlequin Romance

Stranded with the Secret Billionaire
The Billionaire's Christmas Baby
English Lord on Her Doorstep
Cinderella and the Billionaire

Visit the Author Profile page
at Harlequin.com for more titles.

Praise for
Marion Lennox

"What an entertaining, fast-paced, emotionally charged read Ms. Lennox has delivered in this book…. The way this story started had me hooked immediately."
—*Harlequin Junkie* on *The Baby They Longed For*

CHAPTER ONE

HE'D MISS HIS plane if he didn't hurry.

Dr Marcus Pierce was on Gannet Island under pressure. Three weeks before she'd died, his mother had gripped his hand and pleaded, 'Marc, please scatter my ashes from Lightning Peak. It's the most beautiful place in the world, the place where I found comfort when I knew I had to leave your father. You were at boarding school, so I knew you were old enough to cope, but it was hard on me. That first Christmas I hiked up there to watch the sunset and I knew I'd done the right thing. Can I die knowing I'll be resting back there this Christmas?'

Despite the strains on their relationship—sometimes he'd even thought, *What relationship?* because surely he'd learned independence when he was a child—there was no way he could refuse such a plea. But his mother might have found an easier peak, Marc decided as he fought his way along the little used bush path. There were plenty of scenic spots near Sydney. Spots that didn't involve a long flight in a small plane, a rugged hike up an overgrown path he wasn't too sure of, and then another rush to catch the plane home again.

But as he watched his mother's ashes settle in the bushland around him, as he soaked in the salt-filled sea breeze and gazed down at the tiny town beneath him and the ocean beyond, he had to acknowledge this place was breathtakingly lovely.

Lightning Peak was almost at the top of the mountain. Moisture was slipping from above, forming a waterfall dropping to a pool of crystal-clear water. The only sound was the splash of water as it hit the pool and then found its way into some unknown underground stream.

He was sitting on a rock looking out at seemingly the whole world. Behind him was a haven for animals, a waterhole in this most unexpected of places.

Gannet was the largest of a group of six gorgeous, semi-tropical islands—the Birding Isles—set far out in the Pacific Ocean. This island in particular had been a healing place for his mountain climbing mother. Louise had been a doctor, an academic researcher. She was highly intelligent but, apart from her disastrous attempt at marriage and motherhood, she was intensely solitary. He could see why Louise had loved it.

There was, however, little time for reflection. His return flight to Sydney left in three hours. Today was Tuesday, and on Thursday he was due to fly to Switzerland. He needed to tie up loose ends at the hospital tomorrow, and pay a couple of cursory Christmas visits to elderly aunts. He needed to get down this mountain now.

He turned—but then he hesitated.

There were three paths leading from the rock platform where he stood.

Actually, they weren't proper paths—they looked more like desire lines for the animals that drank from this rock pool. He hadn't come up the main mountain path, but a side track his mother knew.

'The main lookout's gorgeous but my favourite place is where the water is, on the other side of the mountain,' his mother had told him. 'The path's overgrown—hardly anyone knows about it—but I'll draw you a map. You can't miss it.'

He'd taken care, following her shaky instructions and hand-drawn map to the letter.

When you reach the massive lightning-hit split rock, walk around it and you'll find the path continues. Then there's a Norfolk pine half a kilometre along where the path diverges. Keep left...

He'd reached the rocky platform he was now standing on with a feeling of relief. Turning now though... Which trace of a path had he used when he'd arrived? He'd been so relieved to make it he hadn't noticed.

He glanced again at Louise's map. Close though she'd been to death, her mind had still been sharp, and her instructions to climb to the peak were brilliant.

Her instructions to descend…not so much. She'd have expected him to notice.

He should have noticed. The omission annoyed him. Dr Marcus Pierce was a cardiac surgeon at the top of his field, and his normal setting was one of intelligence, incisiveness and surety.

He wasn't sure now—and he didn't have time to miss his plane.

So think. All the paths had to go down, he reasoned. If he chose the middle one then surely it'd join with the main track somewhere below.

He checked his phone, and even though he was now officially on leave he saw he'd been contacted. He and his friends had booked to fly to Switzerland on Thursday night. The plan was to arrive on Christmas Eve—Saturday—for two weeks of skiing at St Moritz. He was therefore off-duty but, no matter where he was, the medical calls didn't stop.

In honour of his mother he'd switched his phone to silent, so now he had scores of queued messages. The sight was normal, grounding. It reminded him that he was a surgeon who didn't have time for indecision.

But still he stood with his phone in his hand, fighting unusual qualms. He had an urge to ring Kayla. Kayla was a radiologist, a colleague, part of his friendship group about to head to Switzerland. For the last few months they'd been intermittently dating.

But their relationship was fun more than deep, and Kayla was practical. She'd have thought he was overly sentimental if he'd told her what he was doing. Maybe she was right. His isolated childhood had taught him emotion only got in the way of calm good sense, and there was no use phoning her now when calm good sense was all that was needed.

He was wasting time. The middle path seemed more used than the other two.

Go.

Lightning Peak was Dr Elsa McCrae's happy place. Her place of peace. Her place where she could say to patients, *'Sorry, I'm up on Lightning Peak, you'll have to contact Grandpa.'*

She couldn't say it too often these days. At seventy-eight, her grandpa was slowing down. Robert McCrae was unable to cope with the demands of being a doctor on his own, and she tried to spare him as much as she could, but every so often a woman just needed 'me' time.

For once her afternoon clinic had finished early. It was Wednesday, only four days until Christmas. From now on her life would be packed, with patients thinking every last niggle had to be sorted before Christmas Day itself. Then there was Boxing Day, with the usual influx of patients with injuries from new toys, or islanders who'd eaten far too much the day before. She had a queue of things she should be doing right now—there were always things—but her need to get away had been overwhelming. This would be her only chance to regroup before the rush.

She reached the peak after a solitary two-hour climb, checked her phone to make sure there were no catastrophes back in town, then sat on the massive rock platform, looking out to sea. And let her mind drift.

The other five islands that formed the Birding Isles were dots in the distance. Five hundred kilometres away—well out of sight—lay Australia, Sydney, where the evac team came from, where her patients went when she couldn't help them here. There were no doctors on the other islands. Fishing boats took patients back and forth at need—or took Elsa to them—but, apart from her grandfather, Sydney was her closest medical backup.

Last week a visiting tourist had had a major heart attack. She'd somehow hauled him back from cardiac arrest, but he'd arrested again and died before the medevac team had arrived. If he'd been closer to a major cardiac unit… If she'd had colleagues to help…

'Stop it,' she told herself. If she wasn't here there'd be no one at all. Grandpa was failing, and there were no bright young doctors hammering on the door to take up such a remote and scattered practice. What was needed was some sort of integrated medical facility, with means to transfer patients easily between the islands, but the cost of that would be prohibitive. Money was a huge problem.

An hour's boat ride across to an outer island, a couple of hours treating a patient and organising evacuation, an hour's boat ride back—how could she charge islanders anywhere near what that was worth? She couldn't. Her medical practice was therefore perpetually starved for funds, with no financial incentive for any other doctor to join her.

She loved this island. She loved its people and there'd never been a time she'd thought of leaving. It'd break her grandpa's heart and it'd break her heart, but sometimes—like now—she wouldn't mind time away. Christmas shopping in the big department stores. Crowds of shoppers where no one knew her. Bustle, chaos, fun.

A boyfriend who wasn't Tony?

Tony definitely wasn't the one. After just one date he'd explained the very sensible reasons why they should marry, and he'd been proprietary ever since. He made no secret of his intentions and the islanders had jokingly egged him on. Of course she'd said no, and she'd keep saying no, but the pool of eligible guys on the island was depressingly small.

Sometimes she even found herself thinking she could—should?—end up with Tony. Or someone like Tony.

'You have to be kidding. No one I've dated in the whole time I've been here makes my toes curl,' she told the view, and her dopey beagle, Sherlock, came sniffing back to make sure she was okay.

'I'm fine,' she told the little dog, but she lifted him up and hugged him, because for some reason she really needed a hug. Last week's death had shattered her, maybe even more so because she knew her grandfather had heart problems. Plus he had renal problems. She was just…alone.

'But I'm not alone,' she told Sherlock fiercely, releasing him again to head into his sniffy places in the undergrowth. 'I have Grandpa. I have you.

Even if I'm not going to marry Tony, I have the whole of the Birding Isles.'

'Who all depend on me,' she added.

'Yeah, so why are you here staring into space when they need you back in town?' she demanded of herself. 'What dramas am I missing now?'

She rose reluctantly and took a last long look at the view, soaking in the silence, the serenity, the peace. And then she turned to leave.

'Sherlock?' she called and got a sudden frenzied barking in return.

He was well into the bushes, investigating one of the myriad animal tracks that led from this point. He'd have some poor animal cornered, she thought—a wombat, a goanna. A snake?

She wasn't too fussed. Sherlock might be dumb, but he knew enough to stay out of darting distance from a snake, and he never hurt anything he'd cornered. Her dog was all nose and no follow through, but once he'd found the source of a scent he wouldn't leave it. Sighing, she reached into her pocket for his lead and headed into the bush after him.

But she went carefully. This was cave country. The water from the falls had undercut the limestone, and crevices and underground river routes made a trap for the unwary. Her grandpa had taught her the safe routes as a kid, and Sherlock's barking was well off the path she usually followed.

But by the sound of his frenzied barking he wasn't too far, and she knew the risks. She trod carefully, stepping on large rocks rather than loose undergrowth, testing the ground carefully before she put her weight on it.

Sherlock's yapping was reaching a crescendo—whatever he'd found had to be unusual. Not a 'roo then, or a wombat or koala. She wondered what it could be.

'Sherlock?' she yelled again in a useless attempt to divert him.

But the response left her stunned. It was a deep male voice, muffled, desperate.

'Help. Please help.'

He was stuck. Uselessly stuck. Hurting. Helpless.

He'd broken his leg and dislocated his shoulder. The pain was searing, but his predicament almost overrode the pain.

He was maybe fifteen feet down from the chink of light that showed the entrance to the underground chamber into which he'd fallen. The hole must have been covered with twigs and leaf litter, enough to cover it, enough for small animals to cross. Enough to think he was following a proper path.

He'd been moving fast. There'd been a sickening lurch as his boot had stepped through the fragile cover, and an unbelievable sensation as the entire ground seemed to give way. Then the freefall. The agony of his leg buckling underneath him. A searing pain in his shoulder.

And then fear.

He was on rock and dirt, on an almost level floor. He could see little except the light from the hole he'd made above him. The rest of the cave was gloomy, fading to blackness where the light from the hole above cut out.

He'd dropped his phone. He'd had it in his hand, but had let it go to clutch for a hold as he'd fallen. Maybe it was down here but he couldn't find it, and whenever he moved the pain in his leg and shoulder almost made him pass out. He could contact no one.

No phone. No light. Just pain.

According to his watch he'd been underground for twenty-seven hours. He'd dozed fretfully during the night but the pain was always with him. Today had stretched endlessly as he'd fought pain, exhaustion, panic.

He was unbelievably thirsty.

He was finding it hard to stay awake.

He was going nuts.

He'd been calling but he did it intermittently, knowing the chances of being heard in such a place were remote. The effort of calling was making him feel dizzy and sick. He knew he had to harness his resources, but what resources? He had nothing left.

And when could he expect help?

First rule of bushwalking—advise friends of dates and routes. He'd told Kayla he had family business to sort from his mother's death and he was turning his phone off for twenty-four hours. He hadn't told anyone he was flying all the way to Gannet Island.

Panic was so close…

And then, through the mist of pain and exhaustion, he heard a dog. The dog must have sensed he was down here—it was going crazy above him.

And then, even more unbelievably, he heard a woman calling, 'Sherlock!'

Don't go to her.

It was a silent plea to the dog, said over and over in his head as he yelled with every ounce of strength he possessed and tried to drag himself closer to the hole.

'Help… Don't come close—the ground's unsafe—but please get help.'

Elsa froze.

She knew at once what must have happened. Someone had fallen into one of the underground caverns.

Instinct would have had her shoving her way

through the undergrowth to reach whoever it was, but triage had been drilled into her almost from the first day in med school.

First ensure your own safety.

Sherlock was barking in a place that was inherently unsafe. Her little beagle was light on his feet, used to following animal tracks. Elsa, not so much. She'd be dumb to charge off the path to investigate.

She stood still and called, as loud as she could, 'Hey! I'm here. Where are you?'

Sherlock stopped barking at that, seeming to sense the import of her words, and here came the voice again.

'I've fallen underground. Be careful. It looks... it looks like a path but it's not. The ground's unstable.'

'I'm careful,' she called, making her words prosaic and reassuring as possible. 'I'm a local. A doctor. Are you hurt?'

'Yes.' She could hear pain and exhaustion in his tone, and his words were cracking with strain. 'Broken leg and... I think...dislocated shoulder. I fell...through yesterday.'

Yesterday. To lie wounded in the dark for so long...this was the stuff of nightmares.

Next step? Reassurance.

'Okay, we're on it. I'll call for backup and we'll

get you out of there,' she called back. 'It might take a while but help's coming.'

'Thank…thank you.'

But his words faded badly, and she wondered how much effort it had cost him to call out.

'Is your breathing okay?' she shouted. 'Are you bleeding? Do you have water?'

No answer.

'Hello?'

Silence.

Had he drifted into unconsciousness? Collapsed? Was he dying while she stood helplessly above?

Triage, she told herself fiercely. She was no use to anyone if she panicked.

She flipped open her satellite phone, dependable wherever she went, either here or on the outer islands. Her call went straight through to Macka, Gannet Island's only policeman.

'Elsa. What's up?' Macka was in his sixties, big, solid, dependable. He'd been a cop here for as long as Elsa could remember, and the sound of his voice grounded her.

'I'm up on Lightning Peak, following the back path around to the east, almost to the top,' she told him. 'Sherlock's just found someone who's fallen into an underground cavern.'

There was a moment's pause. Macka would know straight away the gravity of the situation.

'Alive?'

'I heard him call but he's been stuck since yesterday.'

'You're safe yourself?'

'Yeah, but I need to go down. He's stopped answering and his breathing sounded laboured. I have basic stuff in my backpack.'

'Elsa…'

'It's okay. I have a decent rope and it was you who taught me to rappel.'

'Wait for us.'

'I can't. It'll take you a couple of hours to reach us. The light'll fail before you get here and I don't know how bad he is. Macka, I'll turn on location sharing on my phone. Can you take a screenshot now so you know exactly where I am? I'm not sure if this phone will work underground.'

'It should, but Elsa…'

'I can't see that I have any other choice,' Elsa said, hearing his deep concern. 'But I'll stay safe, you know I will. And Sherlock will be up top— he'll bark when he hears you.'

'Elsa, please wait for us.'

'But it sounds like he's lost consciousness,' she said, almost gently. Macka's first concern was always to protect her—there was still a part of him that thought of her as the kid who'd landed on the island as a neglected seven-year-old. But she was all grown up now, and triage told her what she was doing was sensible. 'I need to go down and see what's going on, but I'll take every care. Can you let Grandpa know what's happening? Tell him it's under control, though. Don't scare him.'

'I wouldn't dare,' Macka said, and she heard the hint of a rueful smile. 'Anything you say, Elsa.'

'Hey, I'm not that bossy.'

'Reckon you are,' he said, and she heard another smile. Then, in a different tone, 'Reckon you've had to be. But be careful.'

'Same to you,' she told him. 'Don't come up here alone; bring a couple of the guys from the fire station.'

She heard the trace of a chuckle at that. 'Hey, you know Tony's a volunteer. He'll want to come.'

'Yeah, like that'll help,' she said wryly, thinking of staid, solid Tony who'd been acting more and more possessive without any encouragement. 'Macka, do me a favour and don't tell him.'

'This is Gannet, love. This news'll be all over the island before you even disconnect.'

'Fine,' she said wearily. 'Bring the cavalry then. Only Macka, be careful yourselves. This place is dangerous.'

'Don't I know it,' he said grimly. 'Okay, love, let's make sure I have this screenshot with co-ordinates so I know exactly where you are, and get this rescue underway.'

CHAPTER TWO

ELSA HAD BEEN back on the island, working as a doctor, for five years now, and in that time she'd learned to be self-sufficient. The Birding Isles were a speck of six islands in the middle of the Pacific Ocean. They formed a tourist paradise, and tourists sometimes did stupid things. The permanent population of Gannet was seven hundred, but the numbers swelled dramatically over the summer months, and both tourists and locals quickly learned who Elsa was.

She was Doc, and she was fair game. Always. Her latest heart sink had happened only this morning in the general store, in a tiny sliver of time she'd managed between seeing patients. She'd been choosing rolls of Christmas wrapping paper when one of the local fishermen had approached her, hauled off his boot, stood on one leg and held up a grubby foot.

'Reckon me toe's rotten, Doc,' he'd told her, swaying on one leg as the other shoppers had backed away in disgust. 'Pus's been coming out for two days now.'

It was indeed infected. She'd told him to replace his boot and meet her at the surgery. Thankfully, Mae, the owner of the shop, had yelled after her, 'How many of these rolls do you want, Doc?' and a dozen rolls of garish crimson paper had landed on her desk an hour later.

The locals were great, but this type of interruption happened to her all the time. She'd try to go for a swim and someone would yell, 'Doc, the lady over here's got a fish hook stuck in her arm...' Or, 'Doc, a kid's just done a header into a sandbank. Hurt his neck...'

The nurses at the tiny Gannet hospital and on the outer islands were skilled and professional. Her grandfather still did what he could, but she was always first on call.

Like now. She'd slipped away for a last break before the Christmas rush, and she had to rescue someone down a hole.

But she was always prepared. The advantage of being accustomed to urgent calls wherever she went was that she always carried a basic backpack. Small things but vital. A satellite phone. A water bottle. Bandages, antiseptic, adrenaline, antihistamine, glucagon, morphine. She'd almost forgotten what it felt like to walk around without her gear, and she blessed it now.

If she got down the hole, she had supplies that might help.

And she had rope too. This island was a climber's paradise. Most climbers knew their stuff, but it was also a fabulous place for a family holiday. She'd had emergency calls before. 'Doc, there's a kid stuck on a ledge ten feet down with a split knee...'

During her island childhood she'd learned to climb well, and it was often safer and faster to climb to whatever drama was playing out rather than wait for Macka's team.

So she had what she needed, a light, strong rope that looped permanently around the sides of her backpack.

She formed an arrow of stones on the path, backup to show rescuers where she was. Then she headed into the bush, towards the sound of Sherlock's barking, moving from rock to rock, testing each one before she shifted her weight. When the rocks ran out, ten feet before the spot where Sherlock was peering down, she looped the cord around a solid eucalypt. Then she inched further, testing and retesting, until she reached the break in the ground.

It was easy enough to see what had happened. This looked like part of an animal path. Trodden leaf litter lay on either side of a gaping hole where someone had obviously slipped, clutched in vain, then fallen. The surface of leaf litter had obviously held up for light-footed native animals. For a man, not so much.

As she neared the hole she lay on her stomach and inched forward, testing all the way. Using her phone's torch she peered down into the darkness, but she could see nothing. She had another stronger torch, attached to her belt with a carabiner. She fumbled it free and peered again.

She could make out the floor of the cave, maybe fifteen feet down. She couldn't see the man who'd called out.

'Hello?'

Nothing.

Sherlock was on his stomach as well, quivering with excitement, trying to lick her face as she peered down.

'You found him. Well done, boy,' she told him, 'but you're going to have to stay up top and wait for the cavalry.'

She'd have to rappel. Rappelling without a harness was not her favourite thing—for a start the cord would hurt like hell as she'd need to form a makeshift 'seat'. It'd cut into her waist and groin, but there was no avoiding it. With luck, the guys up top would provide her with a decent harness to haul her back up again.

But that was for later. For now she headed back to the tree, fastening her cord as she needed, taking both ends, tying them around her waist, then looping the cord between her legs to form a system where she could safely control her descent.

To Sherlock's disgust she attached him to the same tree. 'Stay,' she told him, and he looked at her with disbelief.

What? I found him and you won't let me come?

One swift pat and she left him, returning to the hole, moving backwards, then leaning back, testing the strength of her rope, testing her control.

Sherlock was staring after her in concern.

'Needs must,' she told him, with a forced attempt at cheer. 'You do dumb things because you're a dog. Me, I'm a doctor, and that means I get to do things that are even dumber.'

And on that note she backed carefully over the lip of the hole and started her descent.

Rappelling on thick flax rope was relatively easy. Rappelling on thin cord was entirely different. The cord did indeed dig into her pelvis and her waist, and her hands struggled to keep their grip. But she managed.

She'd checked out all sides of the hole and figured the side she was on looked the most stable—the last thing she wanted was for the hole to suddenly enlarge, throwing dirt and rock onto the man below. She moved with infinite care, inching her way. It would have been less painful to move faster, but losing control could mean disaster.

She edged into the hole, catching a last glimpse

of a concerned Sherlock before she was in the darkness of the cavern.

She had no hands free to hold her phone, and she'd had to reattach her mini torch to her belt. The light from the torch swung in all the wrong directions. What she needed was a headlamp. Her legs sought for a foothold and found none.

Five feet. Ten.

And at fifteen she finally felt solid rock.

Still she kept the strain on her rope rather than putting her weight on the ground.

She hung in her makeshift harness, fighting back pain as she grabbed her torch again.

There was a mound of leaf litter under her—that must have fallen from above—but the cave stretched out into darkness. The floor was strewn with rocks, dusty grey. At least it seemed solid.

And there he was. The man lay slumped, seemingly lifeless, slightly to the side of where she hung. Her heart hit her boots as she saw him, but as the torchlight hit his face he stirred, winced, then raised his hand to hide his eyes from the beam.

He was a big guy, tall, lean, muscled, built like many of the rock climbers who loved this place.

He didn't look like a rock climber, though. He was wearing fawn chinos and a short-sleeved shirt that wouldn't be out of place in an informal business meeting. His face was framed with short dark hair, dust and an impressive after-five shadow. A trickle of dried blood ran across his forehead and down to his cheek. Still she had the impression of inherent strength.

As he lowered his hand and looked at her, the impression of strength deepened. His piercing eyes surveyed her, as if she was the patient rather than him.

But he *was* the patient and he'd obviously just surfaced from unconsciousness.

She'd done a fast assessment of the cave now. The ground seemed safe enough. She undid her makeshift harness, looped it, tied it to her belt—the last thing she wanted was to lose it, leaving her stuck here—and stooped to examine her patient.

He opened his mouth to speak, failed the first time and then tried again. 'You can't be real,' he managed. 'An...angel?'

'You guessed it. I'm an angel in scruffy jeans and a torn windcheater, with a daft dog barking his head off up top. An angel? Give me a minute while I figure where I put my wings.'

He managed a smile. Almost.

'Hey, I'm not a vision,' she told him, aware that, despite the piercing gaze, what this guy most needed was reassurance. 'I'm Elsa McCrae— Dr McCrae.' She reached for his wrist and was relieved to feel a steady heartbeat. Fast but not scary fast. 'And you?'

'Marcus Pierce,' he told her, struggling to get the words out. 'M... Marc.' His throat sounded thick, clogged. 'Also... I'm also a doctor.'

'Hey, how about that? A colleague?' Fat lot of good that'd be doing you down here, though, she thought. 'Does your neck hurt? Your back?'

'No. Just...my leg. And my shoulder.'

She'd already seen his leg. It lay twisted under him. And his shoulder? It was at the wrong angle. Dislocated? Ouch.

'Your head?' She was looking at the blood on his face.

'I hit it on the way down.' He winced. 'It's nothing. Didn't knock me out.'

'You fainted just now.'

'I never...faint.'

She fixed him with a look. If he was indeed a colleague, he'd know that was nonsense. 'You're lying. Everyone faints, given the right circumstances,' she told him. 'You certainly seem to have lost consciousness after you talked to me earlier.'

'I tried to drag myself under the hole so you'd see me,' he managed grimly. 'Stupid.'

'Yes, because if you'd succeeded I could have landed on you when I climbed down.' She was making her voice deliberately cheerful, deliberately matter-of-fact. 'So passing out was a good thing. It seems your body is more sensible than your head. So lie still now while I see what's what.'

He closed his eyes. Just how much pain are you in? she wondered.

But first things first. Carefully she checked his neck, his movement, his vision. She tested his hands. 'Squeeze please.' She checked his good leg. 'Wriggle your toes?' His good arm. 'Squeeze my fingers.'

He squeezed and held for longer than he needed. She got that. He must have been lying here terrified.

But what she was finding was reassuring. No obvious head injury. No spinal damage as far as she could see. Just the leg and shoulder. And the fact that he was trapped underground.

Next?

She took her water bottle from her backpack and gently raised his head. His eyes flew open.

'Water,' she said, and got a flash of gratitude so great it almost overwhelmed her.

She held the bottle to his mouth. Half the bottle went down before he paused, wiping his mouth, sinking back with a grunt of thanks.

'If you knew how good that tasted…'

'I guess I do. You fell down yesterday? You've had nothing to drink since then?'

'I had a bottle in my bag,' he told her. 'I think... my bag fell with me but I can't see where it is. I tried to search...'

He didn't have to explain further. To drag himself around this rock-filled cavern in the dark with a broken leg... His face was etched with pain; his voice didn't disguise it.

'If it's down here then I'll find it,' she told him, still with that careful cheerfulness. 'But let's get you something for the pain first. Any allergies? If you're a doctor you'll know the drill. Anything I should know about?'

'You don't have morphine?' he asked, incredulous, and she gave him a modest smile, which was probably wasted given that she was working only with the beam of her torch and she was shining the torch on him. To him she must merely be a shadow.

But that was her job, to be a professional, reassuring shadow. 'I'm a Girl Scout from way back,' she told him. 'I was raised to Be Prepared. Brown Owl would be proud of me.'

'I'm proud of you,' he murmured, sinking back on the hard ground. 'No allergies. Feel free to give me as much as you have.'

She didn't. She'd been stuck before, on a ledge where she'd abseiled down, waiting for a helicopter to take an injured kid off. There'd been a five-hour wait and the kid had needed a top-up.

She'd needed to keep some in reserve then, and she might need to do the same now. They might well be stuck here for hours. Or longer.

Her mind was racing now but, wherever it raced, she couldn't see a safe way out of here until morning. They'd need a stretcher and they'd need secure fastenings up top. The closest stable land was thirty feet from the hole. They'd increase the risk of ground collapsing if they weren't working in daylight. She'd definitely need her reserves of morphine.

She didn't say any of that, though. She swabbed his thigh, injected the drug, then carefully sliced away the torn leg of his jeans so she could see what she was dealing with.

That the leg was broken was obvious. She'd seen the rough stones under the entrance hole and thought he must have landed on those. The impact and falling awkwardly would have been enough to snap the bones.

But it wasn't all bad. She touched his ankle and was relieved to feel warmth, plus a pulse. 'Great news, your foot's still breathing,' she told him, taking him at his word that he was a doctor. It didn't take much medical training to know that a break could cut blood supply, and twenty-four hours without would mean dire consequences. 'But the leg does look broken.'

'Of course it's broken,' he growled. 'I couldn't

have this degree of pain without a break. How badly?'

'I'm not sure,' she confessed. 'It doesn't look too bad from where I'm standing. When the morphine kicks in I'll check your toes.'

'Check 'em now.'

'No.' She wasn't having him passing out again. 'If you can bear it, just lie back and see if you can relax until that pain relief kicks in. Then I'll cut off your boot and check your shoulder. It looks dislocated—maybe fractured…'

'I think dislocated,' he told her.

'You might be right, but let's not investigate until the morphine's had time to work. Meanwhile I need to summon the troops. Lie back and think of England while I organise me a posse.'

There was silence at that, and she could almost see his mind sifting her words.

'A posse?' he said at last, sounding cautious. 'You mean…you're on your own?'

'I have my dog. Me and Sherlock.'

'But you've climbed down here without backup.'

'I'm not an idiot,' she told him, hearing alarm. He'd gone straight to the scenario of two people stuck down here rather than one. 'First, I've used a secure rappelling loop, so I can get out again whenever I want. Carrying you with me, not so much, but I've covered that too, because secondly I've already let people know where I am and what I'm doing. Which I'm guessing you haven't?'

'No,' he said ruefully. 'I know, it was incredibly stupid of me, but it's too late to do anything about it now.'

'Don't worry about it,' she told him, thinking though that he was right to feel dumb. Didn't he realise just how close to total disaster he'd been? But she guessed he already knew that. He'd had more than twenty-four hours to think about it. 'Our lovely Sergeant of Police and his troops will probably already be on their way,' she told him, keeping her voice brisk and cheerful. 'I just need to update them on what's needed.'

'So…' He looked as if he was struggling to get his head around what was happening. 'You're not part of a search party already looking for me?'

'Afraid not. Will anyone be wondering where you are?'

'No.' Blunt. Harsh.

'Then that's what you get for not letting anyone know you're here. Downside—no one knows you're here.'

'You think I'm an idiot.'

'Mine's not to judge,' she said primly. Talking was a good way to distract him from pain. 'I just deal with stuff as I find it.'

'And I'm…stuff.'

'I'm sure you're very nice stuff,' she reassured him.

'But idiotic stuff.'

She smiled, hearing the mortification behind his words, but she didn't say anything. It certainly wasn't her place to judge, but he needed to accept that his actions had indeed been foolish.

'So…' he said at last. 'You and your dog were just scouring the mountains looking for any injured…stuff?'

'Sherlock and I found an orphaned wallaby last week,' she told him. 'So yeah, I guess that's us. Like St Bernards in the snow.' She wrinkled her nose. 'And that needs an apology. I forgot to attach the brandy keg around Sherlock's neck. The wallaby didn't need it, but here… Total fail. We'll be crossed off the Worldwide Beagle Rescue Association forthwith.'

He was looking dazed, struggling to follow the flippancy she was using to distract him until the morphine kicked in. 'So Sherlock's…a beagle?'

'Yes he is, and he found you. You owe him a month's supply of dog treats.'

'Who the hell are you?' It was almost a snap.

'Ooh, that's supposed to be my question.' She thought she wasn't doing such a bad job of distracting him. 'Drat, I have a whole questionnaire for new patients back at the surgery. Where's my form when I need it? But I already told you I'm a doctor. Elsa McCrae. FRACGP. General Practitioner. And you?'

'Marcus Pierce,' he responded. 'FRACS. FRACP. Cardiologist.'

FRACS—College of Surgeons. FRACP—College of Physicians. 'A heart surgeon,' she said, imbuing her voice with deferential awe. Thinking, though, that it was so often the intelligent ones that got themselves into dire trouble on the island. Smart didn't always equate to sensible, but she kept her voice neutral. 'That's great,' she told him. 'As soon as the morphine kicks in I'll get you to keep track of your pulse while I check your shoulder and take your boot off. Marcus, will anyone be out looking for you?'

'No.' A flat veto.

'You don't have friends on the island?'

'I came here to scatter my mother's ashes,' he said tightly. 'Privately.'

'I'm sorry,' she said, more gently. 'Did your mother live here?'

'She visited frequently. She loved this peak.'

She sat back on her heels, frowning. Thinking of his name. Pierce. Making associations.

Remembering a little lady with a fierce determination to climb every peak on the island. A lady who'd had to come to see her the last time she was on the island because she couldn't stop coughing. 'I know what's wrong with me, girl,' she'd said when Elsa had listened to her chest. 'I'm a doctor myself. There's nothing you can do to cure me. I just want something to alleviate the symptoms so I can climb Lightning Peak one last time.'

'Louise Pierce?' she said now, even more gentle. 'Was Louise your mum?'

'I...yes.'

'I knew her. She spent a lot of time here, at the Misses Harnett's guesthouse, and we were so sorry when we heard she'd died.' She sighed. 'I know it's easy to be wise after the event, but Rhonda and Marg Harnett were your mother's friends. They would have come up here with you in a heartbeat.'

'I didn't want complications,' he growled. 'I came on yesterday morning's plane and I was intending to be out on the evening plane.'

'And now you have more complications than you could have imagined.' She sighed again. 'I'm so sorry. But I need you to shush now while I try my phone and see if I can get reception from down here.'

She phoned and the satellite did her proud. The line crackled and broke but Macka heard her. 'It's up to you,' she told him. 'But I can't think it'll be safe to bring him up until dawn. Can you bring us a decent lamp, pillows, rugs and maybe a couple of air mattresses? I have a rappelling loop set up so we can lower stuff. Oh, and can you bring some dog food for Sherlock?' Her dog had ceased barking but she knew he'd be waiting patiently above ground and wanting his dinner.

She disconnected and turned to find Marcus looking mortified. 'Morning?'

'Sorry, but I don't think it's safe to bring you up until we have decent light.'

'Hell,' he said. And then, 'There's no need for you to stay down here too.'

'You know there is,' she said matter-of-factly. 'You've done the medical training. You know the rules.'

'I won't have blood clots. I won't pass out again.'

'Yeah, but I didn't bring the indemnity forms,' she told him. 'And it's no problem. Because of the remoteness of this island I did extra training as an emergency doctor. Rappelling into caves and being stuck underground will add enormous credit to my CV.'

She was swinging her torch beam around the floor as she talked. She found his phone first. Smashed in the fall. Thank God for Sherlock's hunting instincts, she thought. Without his phone he could have lain here until…

No. It didn't bear thinking about.

She also found a good-looking leather slouch

bag, which held a wallet and, wonderfully, another bottle of water. On the strength of it she offered Marcus more.

He drank with gratitude. Despite the greyness of his face as she'd shown him his smashed phone—he must realise what he'd been facing even more acutely than she did—he was looking less rigid. The morphine must be taking effect.

'Right,' she said briskly as he settled again—or settled as much as anyone could on dirt and rocks— 'let's get you to work. Cardiac surgeon? I don't need the surgeon part so much, but can you keep track of your pulse while I get this boot off?'

He even managed a chuckle at that, a deep, nice chuckle, another great sign that the morphine was working.

Leg first. The shoulder needed attention but blood supply to the foot had to be her first concern.

She headed for his boot, blessing the sharp little everything tool she always carried. Yes, his ankle had a pulse, but she wanted to see pink toes. His foot was swollen—she'd expect nothing else with the damage to his leg—and the boot alone could now be constricting supply.

'So, your job…' he said, and she could hear the strain in his voice as she took her time to slice the thick, good quality leather. 'You're on permanent patrol up here? Is that how you make a living? Donations from the grateful lost? How many hikers do you find?'

'More than you might think,' she told him, remembering previous island walks interrupted as she'd come across lacerations, sprained ankles, insect bites—and, more recently and more dreadfully, the full-blown cardiac arrest.

She could have used a cardiac surgeon then, she thought bleakly. She'd never felt so alone, so helpless. Specialist help could have saved a life, but it was an ocean away.

'And the rest of the time?' he asked.

'I have a surgery down near the jetty,' she managed, hauling herself from just one of the memories of failure that haunted her. 'We have a hospital too. It serves all the islands. It's mostly used for our elderly—six of our ten beds are classified nursing home. The rest are simple problems—minor infections, patients waiting for evacuation to Sydney or continuing their recovery after being transported home. It's a very basic medical service but it's all we can manage.' She had his sock off now and was examining toes. 'Marcus, this is looking good. There can be no blood supply constriction at all.'

'Just the matter of a broken leg and twisted shoulder.'

'There is that,' she said, looking again at the

damage. Thinking of possible movement. Possible consequences. 'Marcus...'

'My friends call me Marc.'

'You might not want to call me a friend when I tell you what I want to do,' she told him. 'That leg's definitely broken and I need to splint it to make sure circulation stays secure. You have lacerations and bruising where it must have struck rock, but nothing's piercing the skin. If I up the morphine and you manage to grit your teeth, I reckon it'll be safer to straighten it a little and brace it. It'll need to be braced before we move you tomorrow anyway, so I might as well do it now. Plus I might as well see if I can get that shoulder into a more comfortable position.' She tried to smile. 'It'll save you lying awake all night worrying about surgery in the morning.'

'You're all heart.' She saw him close his eyes, accept the inevitable. 'How are you at fixing dislocated shoulders?'

'Without an X-ray? I'd normally not even go there.'

'But in an emergency situation? Given the low risk? I've felt it. There's no suspicion of fracture.'

'You can't know that.'

'I felt it as I fell. It twisted hard but not hard enough to break. I'm sure this is a simple dislocation. Elsa, it's agony and I'm done with agony. I tried to put it back myself.'

'Yeah?' Like that was easy to do. 'With what results?'

'I did actually faint,' he admitted. 'So then I stopped.'

'Very wise.'

'But you could do it.'

'I might not be able to.'

'You could try. You're sensible enough to stop if it doesn't click into place fast.'

She sat back and considered. 'You'd accept the risk?'

'Yes, I would.'

There was a level of trust. He'd accepted her as competent enough to do no harm.

'I guess,' she said doubtfully. 'With the morphine on board… I could give you a muscle relaxant too.'

'Bless you,' he said simply and then moved on, almost colleague to colleague. 'The leg. What'll you brace it with?'

'That's the good side about you falling,' she told him, making her voice brisk, as professional as she could. 'We have a selection of bush litter around us. I can see at least three sticks I can whittle with my neat little knife to make a nice smooth brace. You'd have to agree with me though, Marc. You'd have to accept that I'll hurt you.'

He closed his eyes for a moment and then opened them, and his face had become resolute.

'Help me to sit up,' he asked her. 'I need to see my leg for myself first.'

'No.' She put her hands on his chest, firmly pressing him back. 'I know you've been trying to move but Marc, you must know there's the possibility of spinal damage. You fell hard. You know the rules. Let's get you safely X-rayed before you start shifting. We'll get you up on a stretcher and check you before you start doing fancy stuff like sitting up.'

'But...'

'No buts. You know what's sensible.'

He closed his eyes, looking grim. 'I'm supposed to be flying to St Moritz tomorrow, to be there over Christmas,' he muttered. 'For a couple of weeks' skiing.'

She raised her brows at that. 'Really?' She paused to consider. 'I guess it could still happen. How are you at skiing on one leg?'

No answer.

She hadn't really expected one. She thought, tangentially, how amazing to live a life where you could pop over to St Moritz to ski when you felt like it.

He'd be a good skier, she thought. Okay, she didn't know for sure, but she could sense it. His body was solid, muscled, ripped in all the right places.

She was still holding him. She'd moved to stop him shifting and her arm had gone around his good shoulder as she'd tugged him back to a prone position and encouraged him to relax. She'd left her arm there for a moment. He was cold and she was warm. He needed contact.

Comfort?

But the comfort seemed to be working both ways. This underground dungeon was creepy. It was almost dark above them.

She had a phone light and a torch. She had a spare battery for her phone in her backpack. Help was on its way. There was no need for her to want comfort.

But still, as she held him and felt his inherent strength, she took it where she found it. She'd learned to do that. She had her grandpa's help when she needed it medically, but Grandpa was growing increasingly frail. She had Sherlock, but...

But there were still lots of times in Dr Elsa McCrae's medical life when she felt totally alone, and for just one brief moment now she let herself accept the feel of this man beside her. She let herself imagine that maybe she could depend on him.

Which was ridiculous. His mind was clearly

focused on the next thing. Bracing his leg. Thinking about his shoulder.

'Okay,' he said briefly. 'Let's get it over with.'

She hesitated. She could—maybe she should—wait for more light. But it'd still be a couple of hours before help arrived. Macka was a great policeman but he wasn't the fittest bloke on the island. He'd have called on a couple of the fire brigade guys to help. They were fitter, faster than Macka but they didn't know the route.

Two hours. She released him and looked again at that leg and thought it did need to be fixed fast. If it was a compound fracture… She had no way of knowing for sure, and she had to work on the worst-case scenario.

'We do it now,' Marcus said, and she heard her own thoughts reflected in the tone of his voice. He'd know the risks as well as she did. 'And the shoulder if you can. Let's go.'

So she did.

CHAPTER THREE

SHE WAS NO orthopaedic surgeon and she wanted to be one. She had no X-ray equipment and she needed it. She had no help and she wanted that, too.

All she had were her instincts.

Do no harm. First rule in every situation. She had a leg that still had circulation. She could leave it exactly how it was. His shoulder needed to be X-rayed to make sure it wasn't broken. She should leave that in place too.

But a dislocated shoulder was too excruciatingly painful for him to sleep, even with the morphine, and in the morning he had to be moved regardless. The long night lay ahead of them and the shoulder would be agony. And if he moved during the night, if the leg twisted as they tried to get him up, if his circulation blocked… It didn't bear thinking about.

No X-ray machine would miraculously appear down here. No orthopaedic surgeon was on his way with Macka. She was on her own.

So what was new? She'd coped before, and she'd cope again.

She could have waited until Macka arrived with better light but what she was doing depended mainly on feel. Plus the cooperation of her patient. If she'd been back at the hospital she'd use general anaesthetic. She couldn't use it here but, blessedly, Marc's medical training would have him understanding the absolute imperative of keeping still.

Leg first. The shoulder was more painful, but the risk of blocked circulation to the foot meant it was triaged first.

She prepared one of the pieces of wood that had been shoved down the hole with the force of Marc's fall. She showed it to Marc, who made a crack about her whittling skills before falling silent again as she worked.

He was mentally preparing himself for what lay ahead, she thought. Morphine could only do so much.

Then, moving more slowly than she'd ever worked before, she inched the wood under his leg. With her hands feeling his leg, feeling for bone, she slowly, slowly straightened his knee, then straightened his leg, manoeuvring it onto her makeshift splint.

She cleaned and disinfected and bandaged and then fixed the leg as tightly as she dared to her whittled wood. Marc said nothing the entire time she worked, and she blessed him for it.

Finally she sat back and took a breath. It was cool and damp underground, but she found she was sweating.

'Well done,' Marc growled softly, and she caught herself. What was she doing sweating, when it was Marc who'd managed to hold himself rigid?

'Well...well done yourself,' she told him. 'I...' She caught herself, giving herself space to find the right words. To find a prosaic normalcy. 'The pulse in your lower leg is stronger. If I keep the morphine for during the night you should be able to sleep without worrying about shifting.'

'So now the shoulder.'

That was harder. She knew it'd mean more pain for him and she was less sure of herself. Heaven, she wanted an X-ray.

The simplest and safest technique for shoulder reduction was the Stimson technique, where the patient hung his or her arm down and weights were attached at the wrist. This was normally her go-to method but here there was no bed, no raised surface. Scapular manipulation also had to be ruled out. Given the possibility of back injury, there was no way she was rolling him into the position required.

Which left external rotation as the next best option. That could at least be done with the patient lying on his back. She talked to Marc as she thought it through. 'You reckon?' she asked him. He was, after all, a colleague—and it was his shoulder.

'Go for it,' he urged.

So she did. With his arm tucked in as close to his body as possible, gently, slowly she rotated, letting gravity—and pain—limit the amount of movement. She watched his face every inch of the way, watching the greyness, the tight set of his mouth, the fierce determination to get this done. As his pain level increased his arm automatically tensed. She backed off, waited, then inched again.

And then, miraculously, wonderfully, came the moment when it slid back into place. She saw his face go slack with relief and knew her own face must reflect it.

'Thank you,' he said, his eyes closed, his whole body seeming to sag. 'Oh, my God, thank you.'

'Think nothing of it,' she managed, and to her disgust heard a tremor in her own voice. 'I'll strap it now. It needs to stay strapped until I get you to where we can check for rotator cuff injury. You must know the drill. Hopefully now though you'll be comfortable enough to get some sleep.'

'Sleep...' He grimaced. 'Look, now we have everything braced, surely I can be pulled up to the surface.'

'Not on my watch.' She had herself back under control now. 'You heard what I said to Macka.

He'll bring stuff to make us more comfortable, but I'm not risking bringing you up until we have decent light.'

'But if my leg's braced...'

'I'm not thinking about you,' she told him, only partly truthfully. 'I'm thinking about the unstable ground and a team up there who aren't trained cavers. I'm thinking about that ground collapsing. I'm thinking about half the Gannet Island fire department landing on our heads.'

'Oh,' he said doubtfully.

'And I've used the last of my bandages,' she told him. 'If a team of burly firefighters fall down here, my emergency kit's going to look pretty darned empty. No. We wait until morning when Macka—he's our island cop and he's good—can do a thorough recce of the ground.'

'Right,' he said, clearly not liking it but reaching acceptance. 'But you could go up. There's no need for both of us to stay down here.'

'Yeah,' she told him, thinking of clots, thinking of delayed concussion, thinking of kinked blood vessels that still might block.

'I can do my own obs.'

That brought a wry smile. 'Really? A specialist cardiologist doing obs? When was the last time you did such a thing? Don't cardiologists have nursing staff for that?'

'You're not a nurse.'

'No, I'm a family doctor in a remote community, and as such I've even done hourly obs on a pregnant turtle. Mind, it was a special turtle and I had her in a sand tank on my veranda but there you go, needs must.'

'Did you have a good outcome?' he asked, distracted as she'd hoped he would be.

'An excellent outcome. Seventy-three babies that we hope went on to become seventy-three of Gannet Island's finest. Never doubt my skill, Dr Pierce. I can do your obs, no problem. There's no need to be scared at all.'

'Believe it or not, I'm not in the least scared,' he told her. 'Not from the moment you slid down your rope.'

'Then I've done my job until now,' she said cheerfully. 'And I'll keep doing it if you don't mind. So you settle down and see if you can sleep and I'll check the whereabouts of the team up top.'

'Elsa…'

'Yep?'

'If any of the team up top fall and break a leg…or if there's an emergency in town tonight… another turtle?'

'Then Grandpa will cope,' she told him, making her voice more sure than she felt.

'Grandpa?'

'He's our other doctor on the island. He's good.'

'How old is he?'

'Seventy-eight.'

'Then…'

'If you're going to be ageist I'll need to report you to the med board for discrimination. Grandpa can cope.'

'But apart from Grandpa…'

'His name's Robert.'

'Apart from Robert, you're the only doctor on the island?'

'I am,' she told him soundly. 'Plus vet and sometimes nurse and sometimes cook and sometimes janitor. General dogsbody, that's me. Grandpa and me and my beagle, Sherlock, together we practically run this island. Now, could you please shush because I need to ring Macka again.'

'Elsa…'

'Shush,' she told him severely. 'You get on with being a patient, Marcus Pierce, and let me get on with being Doctor in Charge.'

Macka's team arrived half an hour later. Sherlock announced their arrival with shrill excited barks—as well he might. These guys were friends and it was way past his dinnertime.

'Is that our rescue team?' Marc had been dozing under the effects of the morphine but the barking and yells above them had him opening his eyes.

'Doc?' Macka called down, strongly authoritative. 'Shut up, Sherlock.'

Amazingly, he did. Macka's word was law on this island.

'We are,' she called up. 'But stay back. The ground's unstable. Can you see where I've tethered my rope? Don't come any closer than that. I want Marc out of here, but not at the cost of another accident. Who's there?'

'Denise and Graham. We can call on more if we need them. How are things down there?'

'Stable,' she told him. 'No need for rush. Don't come any closer, guys. This ground is a trap for the unwary.'

'But you're safe?'

'We're both safe. Marc has a broken leg and an injured shoulder, but we can hold out until it's safe to pull us both up. Marc's going to need a stretcher.'

'We have the rescue stretcher.'

'That's great,' she told him, thinking thankfully of their newly acquired piece of kit, a collapsible stretcher with straps that could hold a patient completely immobile while being shifted. Or, in this case, lifted.

There was still the possibility of damage to Marc's back. First rule of medicine—do no harm.

Shifting him before she could take an X-ray was the stuff of nightmares.

'Can you hold out until first light?' Macka called.

'I think we must.' She wanted a steady ascent, everything in their favour, and if it meant waiting then they had no choice. She was looking at Marc, meeting his gaze, calm and steady. He'd know the options.

'Then we'll hold off,' Macka said, sounding relieved. 'Tell us what's happened?'

She told him. There was silence as he thought things through.

'Right, then. We'll get the gear down to you and set up here. Your guy... Marc? Is there anyone we need to contact on his behalf?'

Marc shook his head, looking grim. 'No one will miss me until tomorrow.'

She frowned at that but Macka was waiting for a reply. 'He says not.'

'Fair enough,' Macka said.

'You want us to ring your grandpa? How about Tony?'

'I'll ring Grandpa,' she called back. 'And don't you dare ring Tony.'

There was a chuckle and then things turned businesslike.

'Okay, we'll use your rope as a pulley and lower enough gear to make you comfortable for the night,' Macka told her. 'We brought the medical supplies you need, plus a couple of air mattresses and blankets. You can set the air mattress below the stretcher so it won't need another shift in the morning. We'll stay up here in case the situation changes but, unless it does, at first light we'll organise a line across to keep us stable, get a stretcher down there and winch you both up.'

'Can you contact the mainland to stand by for an evac flight?' She wanted an orthopaedic surgeon to take over care of this leg, the sooner the better. 'We ought to be able to get him to the airport by late morning.'

'That might be harder,' Macka called back. 'There's bushfires on the mainland and the smoke's affecting all the major airports. Evac flights are detoured up north, but only if they're life or death—they have to come from Brisbane and the fires are keeping them flat-out. Normal commuter flights are already called off for tomorrow. Mae's going nuts because she has an order for forty Christmas turkeys. The way this is looking, they'll be lucky to arrive Boxing Day.'

'No! Five of those turkeys are for us.' She kept her voice deliberately light because the grim look on Marc's face had intensified. Had he still been hoping to make St Moritz?

It was sad about that, but it was tough for her, too. She'd have to take X-rays and set the leg herself. Grandpa would help, but doing such a procedure on someone who wasn't an islander and therefore couldn't be expected to accept the medical limits caused by their remoteness...

She'd worry about that tomorrow, she told herself.

There was a call from above them. A tightly wrapped bundle was descending, tied on her looped rappel rope. First delivery.

She caught it before it reached the ground. A lantern was attached to the side. She flicked it on and for the first time saw the extent of their cavern.

Or, rather, the enormity of it. It stretched downward on all sides. Marc had been so lucky that he'd landed on a site that was almost stable.

She didn't say anything though, just unfastened the bundle.

Two self-filling air mattresses.

'Hey, look at this,' she told him, holding the first up as it inflated. 'Who needs to go to St Moritz for luxury?' She shivered. 'Speaking of which, who needs to go to St Moritz for cold? Did you guys bring blankets?' she called.

'Coming down,' Macka told her, and ten minutes later they had everything they needed to keep themselves if not exactly comfortable, then not too cold and not too uncomfortable.

It took time and skill to move Marc onto the

combined mattress and stretcher but at last he was where he needed to be.

'Done,' she called back up. 'All secure.'

'Then dinner,' Macka called and an insulated bag came down. 'Deirdre's chicken soup and bread rolls. It went in hot so it should still be warm. She figured your guy might be feeling a bit off, so chicken soup might be the ticket.'

'Wow, thank you,' she called back and guided the bag down and nestled it beside the now almost comfortable Marc.

Who was looking at her in disbelief.

'Hot food as well.'

'Gannet Island's all about service,' she told him, smiling. 'Do you think you can drink some? Let me help you. No, don't try and sit up. Just let me support your shoulders while you drink.'

'I can...'

'I'm very sure you can sit up,' she told him severely. 'But you know as well as I do that you risk your leg moving and I'm still worrying about your back. If there's spinal injury... And if that leg loses circulation...' She paused while they both thought of the consequences.

'So you're telling me to lie back, shut up and do what I'm told,' he said, still grim.

'That, Dr Pierce, is exactly what I'm doing, and if you knew how much I, as a family doctor,

have longed to say that to a specialist then you'll
know that this night is not all bad.'

'For who?'

'For me,' she told him and grinned. 'Now shut
up and let's get this soup into you.'

CHAPTER FOUR

MARC LET HER support his shoulders while he drank the soup—for which he was pathetically grateful. For the last twenty-seven hours he'd been in agonising pain. Thirst had broken through, so practically all he'd thought of was fear, water and the pain in his leg and shoulder.

This magical woman had fixed the fear, given him water and made his leg and shoulder little more than dull aches. Now she was pretty much hand-feeding him the most delicious soup he'd ever tasted.

She'd wedged her body under his, sitting on the ground at his head, using her body to prop the pillow of his air mattress higher. There was canvas between them, but it felt as if there was nothing at all. His head seemed to be pillowed on a cushion of warmth and relief and gratitude.

She helped him hold the mug to his lips and he felt the warmth of her hand and he thought he'd never met someone so wonderful in all his life.

'Marry me,' he murmured as he finished the last of his soup and she chuckled.

'That's not even original. There's Tony, who

asks me that once a week, plus I get proposals from whoever else is grateful right now. I was propositioned only yesterday when I lanced old Roger Havelock's abscess. He'd been putting up with it for a week so the relief from pressure was nothing less than sensational. I could have asked for half his kingdom. Not that that's saying anything,' she added reflectively. She shifted back, lowering his pillowed head gently, and he was aware of a sharp stab of loss as she shifted away. 'Roger owns fifteen sows, two boars and a handful of scraggy chickens. Are you offering anything better?'

'Anything better than Tony?'

'I'm not into comparisons.'

'Yet you counted sows as an alternative proposal. Surely that means you're available?'

'I'm always available,' she said, and he heard irony in the tone. 'How about you? I'm assuming your offer of marriage was something you make to every doctor who climbs down a hole to save your life, but seriously… Are you sure you don't have anyone who'll be out of their mind with worry right now?'

'I'm positive,' he said brusquely. 'I don't have any close family and I'm supposed to be on vacation. I'm due to fly to Switzerland tomorrow night with a group of fellow medics. That includes Kayla, a colleague. She'll worry if I don't turn up to the airport without letting her know, but a phone call tomorrow will fix that. Our relationship's only casual. She won't miss me until then, and she'll have a good time without me.'

'I suppose that's a good thing,' she said doubtfully. 'You want to sleep?'

'I guess. You must need to, too.'

'I do, and apart from checking you I might even get a whole night without interruptions.' She hauled her mattress to lie beside his and spread out blankets. 'Maybe I should try this more often—jumping down a hole to get a good night's sleep.'

'Is it so hard to get?'

'Yes, it is,' she said, tucking her blankets around her with care. 'You try being the only full-time doctor for a group of islands where every tourist seems intent on putting themselves in harm's way.'

'Like me.'

'You said it.' She checked out his blankets, twitched another over him and nodded. 'There. Tucked in and settled. Pain level?'

'About two.'

'That'll have to do.'

'It'll do me. Thank you, Elsa.'

'All my pleasure,' she told him. 'Wake me if it gets above three. There are no medals for being a martyr.'

'Are there any medals for being a lone doctor and a heroine to boot?'

'I'm not completely alone,' she said indignantly. 'There's Grandpa. He'd be full-time if I let him but there's the little matter of renal problems and a dicky heart.'

'Renal problems?'

'Diabetes. Not so bad.' Mostly.

'And a dicky heart?'

'That's the diagnosis,' she said lightly. 'I told you I'm a family doctor. Nothing fancy.'

'Surely he's been off the island to find out exactly what's wrong?'

'He has,' she said and lay down and tugged the blankets up to her chin. 'But he hates being off the island. That's the biggest reason I'm here, but I'm not about to discuss Grandpa's health in detail with another patient.'

'I'm a cardiologist.'

'Says you. For now you're my patient. You're suffering a broken leg and sore shoulder, plus a severe case of being stuck down a cave. I suggest you try and sleep, Dr Pierce, before that morphine wears off. Like I intend to.'

'You're going to sleep before my morphine wears off?'

'Exactly. I'm not stupid. If I wait any longer you'll start whinging and I need my beauty sleep.'

* * *

He dozed and then he woke and sleep wouldn't return.

He lay and thought of the complications one broken leg entailed. He thought about his friends heading to St Moritz. He thought of Kayla. He'd told Elsa she'd go to St Moritz without him and of course she would. Their relationship was purely fun and casual. There was no need for her to stay and hold his hand.

This Christmas skiing vacation was an institution between a group of colleagues, something he'd done for six years now. Kayla was simply one of the group, and they'd started dating only recently. Their enjoyment of St Moritz had little to do with each other. They both enjoyed the hard physical challenge, the beauty of the slopes, the crowded bars, the excellent restaurants.

The avoidance of Christmas.

Though it wasn't totally avoided. The resort their small group stayed in took elegance to a whole new level, with sumptuous furnishings, exotic food, magnificent decorations and designer gifts for each guest. They'd arrive on Christmas Eve and the festivities would be in full swing. The setting was picture-perfect, a magical white Christmas full of people enjoying themselves.

As opposed to the Christmases he'd spent during his childhood, with his parents trying unsuccessfully to disguise mutual grievances. Stilted cheer in their harbourfront mansion. Gifts—something aspirational and educational and expensive from his father, something ecologically sound and expensive from his mother.

A part of him had almost been relieved the Christmas his mother had finally left. At ten he'd been old enough to realise that at least it had eased the sham of pretending not to hear the bitter fighting. Afterwards he could take his certificate from his mother saying he'd just donated a school to a village in Africa—surely what every kid wanted for Christmas—and thank her as if he meant it. He could accept his mind-bending educational challenge from his father and not have to figure how to negotiate the minefield of which gift he liked best.

Christmas when his parents were together had been a formal, rigid nightmare. Christmas as a teen when they'd been apart had been something he could almost get through.

Christmas in St Moritz?

Fun. Friendly. Busy.

Impersonal. Which was the way he liked his life.

The group congregating at the airport tomorrow would miss him, but only briefly. He was honest enough to suspect the short-term relationship he'd had with Kayla was pretty much already over. Kayla might even be secretly pleased she'd have a spare seat beside her on the long plane flight.

But then his tired mind drifted sideways. To the woman beside him.

Would a woman like this stay because her man had broken his leg?

She didn't have to tell him she was here on this island because of her commitment to the island-ers and her grandfather—it was implied in almost every word she spoke. As for not talking about what was wrong with her grandfather... Patient confidentiality? Not so much. He was another doctor, a specialist, and the chance to talk to an-other professional about a worrying case would be grabbed by almost every colleague he knew.

Not by Elsa though. In that quick rejoinder about patient confidentiality he'd heard pain. Something grim in the background. Something she didn't need advice about.

Something she already knew? That staying here was putting her grandfather's life at risk?

She'd saved his life. Maybe he could help her in return. He needed to figure this out.

'You need more pain relief?' It was a sleepy murmur from beside him. She'd placed their air mattresses so close they were touching. He knew the reason for that too. He'd had a fall. She had no guarantee that it wasn't only his leg and shoulder that were damaged. If he was in hospital he'd be under constant observation for at least twenty-four hours.

'You know, this is the second night I've been stuck down here,' he told her. 'If I was going to die of internal bleeding I probably would have done it before this. There's no need for you to stay awake.'

'Which is why I'm sleeping.'

'You're awake.'

'So I'm dozing. You're a doctor. You know we can exist on dozes. So how's your pain?'

'Still okay.'

'Bladder?'

Hell, he was a surgeon at the top of his field. The physical dependencies this situation called for were humiliating.

'I'm fine,' he told her dourly and he heard her smile.

'Then drink more. Don't you dare stop drinking because you have too much pride to let me help you. You're a patient, remember.'

'I don't have to like it.'

'What's that quote about being given the serenity to accept things you can't change? I can't remember it exactly, but it's something like "*Grant me the serenity to accept the things I cannot change, courage to change the things I can and wisdom to know the difference.*" My grandpa has it on his wall and it's wise. So if you need the bottle, accept it with serenity.'

'Right,' he said wryly. 'But I don't need it.'

'And I'll accept that you're pig stubborn and we'll leave it at that,' she told him.

They lay in silence for a few moments. He thought she might have dozed off again but then her voice sounded cautiously into the dark.

'Tell me about St Moritz.'

'You've never been?'

'Hey, I've been to Sydney,' she said cheerfully. 'Is there a world past that?'

'Only Sydney?'

'No money to go further,' she told him, still upbeat. 'It took all Grandpa's resources to help me through med school. During vacations I came home and worked for my keep in the hospital. Actually,' she admitted, 'I've worked in the hospital since I was seven. One of my earliest memories is helping shell what seemed like a mountain of peas, but my official job was cheering patients up. Me and Loopy the Basset, then me and Peanut the Fox Terrier and finally me and Sherlock the Beagle—had to go in and find stuff to talk about. It was the best training for family medicine ever.'

'So what about your mum and dad?'

'Mum was your original hippie,' she said, almost curtly. 'My grandmother died when Mum was thirteen and Mum took it hard. She blamed

Grandpa—"You're a doctor, why couldn't you save her?" Then she took up with the surf crowd who come here every summer. She ran away when she was seventeen, following her heart, only the guy her heart had chosen turned out to be a scumbag. Coming back here was never an option for her, though, and she died of an overdose when I was seven. Who knows where my Dad is now?—I certainly don't. After Mum died, Grandpa brought me to the island and, apart from the years in Sydney at med school, I've been here ever since. So I say again…tell me about St Moritz.'

He was silent for a moment, letting himself sink into the story behind the story. He was imagining a neglected child with a drug-addicted mother, a despairing grandfather, grief.

Hell, and he'd thought his childhood was hard.

'St Moritz,' she said again, and he gave himself a mental shake and tried to think of what she'd like to know.

'You've seen all those soppy Christmas cards with snow scenes and twinkling lights and carollers and reindeer…'

'Don't tell me there are reindeer!'

'I believe there are. Not on the ski slopes though, and that's where I mostly spend my time.'

'It's really white? Not just slush?'

'It can get slushy, but at this time of the year,

especially when the snow's just fallen, it's beautiful.'

'I'd so love to see it. They say every snowflake is different. To stand in the snow…to taste snow on my tongue…'

'Would you let me give you a trip there—as payment for saving my life?'

It was the wrong thing to say. He knew it as soon as the words came out of his mouth. She was lying beside him, her arm just touching his. He wasn't close enough to really feel it, but he could sense the sudden rigidity in her. The withdrawal.

'Hey, you're just a patient and I don't need gifts from patients,' she told him, and her words were cool and stiff. 'Tourists have accidents on the island all the time, and it's my job to patch them up. You'll get a bill for services rendered.'

'What, standard consultation with medical procedure attached?'

'More than that,' she said with asperity. 'House call out of hours. Extended consultation. Minor surgery. You'll be slugged heaps.'

'Do you charge more than the government rebate?' he asked, knowing already what her answer would be.

'Even if I did it wouldn't equal a holiday in St Moritz,' she told him. 'Go to sleep.'

'I don't think I can.'

'Try,' she told him curtly and rolled over to face away from him.

And that was that.

Insensitive toe-rag.

A holiday in St Moritz! Grateful patients often gave her chocolates or wine, or nice handwritten cards. She never expected them, but when they came she appreciated them and shared them around with the receptionists and nursing staff. It seemed a thank you to all of them.

A holiday in St Moritz. As if.

But she lay in the dark, and for a little while she let herself imagine what it could be like. A plane ride to Sydney and then an overseas flight to Switzerland. A long flight. She wouldn't be the least surprised—given the insouciance of this guy's offer—if it'd be in business class, too. Then maybe a limo drive to the ski slopes.

Her receptionist had a passion for glossy lifestyle magazines, and they ended up in her waiting room. Occasionally, in the tiny spaces between patients, she let herself browse and dream.

There'd be a chalet—she'd seen the pictures. Luxurious resort suites. Views to die for. Maybe a sauna and a spa. Ski lessons with some gorgeous young Swiss, herself skimming down the ski slopes, then afterwards roaring fires, food and drink at expensive restaurants, laughter among friends…

And that was where the picture cut out. Friends.

She was so damned lonely.

Oh, for heaven's sake, what was she doing thinking she was lonely? She could count on almost every islander as her friend.

How many of them called her Elsa, though? From the time she'd returned to the island she'd been the doctor's kid. The islanders had taken her into their hearts, loved her, cared for her so her grandpa could keep up with his medicine. But mostly Grandpa had cared for her himself. She'd been his shadow and the locals had called her Little Doc. 'Here comes Doc and Little Doc,' they'd say, and if things got tricky then whoever was closest would spirit Little Doc away until she could resume her role as his helper.

So she'd been Little Doc until she'd come back from university, and then she'd been simply, proudly Doc. For Grandpa had never been into money-making, and so the islanders had chipped in to help fund her studies, too.

Grandpa called her Matey. She was Grandpa's mate. Everyone else called her Doc.

Except recently Tony. Tony called her Elsa.

Dating Tony had been a disaster. She should never have agreed to that first date. He'd almost instantly become possessive, and his use of her first name was a claim all by itself.

He'd caught her at a weak moment.

Because she was lonely!

The guy beside her stirred, and she thought she should probably say something to cheer him up. She couldn't think of a single thing.

Instead she lay in the dark and for some unfathomable reason her future lay on her like a thick, heavy blanket.

St Moritz.

Why had one crazy offer disturbed her so much?

Or the way this guy had smiled at her?

He was just another patient. A tourist. He'd be out of here as soon as the smoke cleared enough for flights to resume.

More to distract herself than anything else, she let herself think of the situation on the mainland. What had seemed a series of small fires two days ago had merged into a much bigger front. If she'd been working on the mainland she'd be so busy— part of a team coping with burns, smoke inhalation, shock. Part of a team...

Oh, for heaven's sake, she was thinking longingly of a bushfire situation?

'What's the latest on the fires on the mainland?' Marc's deep growl cut through her thoughts, made her blink. Were his thoughts following hers?

He'd be worried about getting out of here, she thought. Nothing more.

'Latest report says there's light rain,' she told him briefly. 'I guess that's why the smoke's so intense. Slow moisture on burning bushland. No lives lost, though.' She thought about it for a moment. 'If it was worse… Do cardiologists cope with fire trauma?'

'Everyone copes when it's major,' he said simply. 'But if it's settling now I won't be missed. Plus I'm now officially on vacation.'

'Lucky you.'

'You think I'd prefer to be on vacation rather than helping out?'

'Everyone needs a break sometimes,' she said flatly. 'Lucky you if you can get one. Go to sleep, Marc, or at least let me. I'm not on vacation and I need sleep even if you don't.'

CHAPTER FIVE

THE EVACUATION BEGAN the next morning and it nearly killed him that he had to play the victim. The idiot who'd got into such trouble.

He *was* the victim. He *was* the idiot.

So he lay strapped onto his stretcher while they worked around him.

The inflatable stretcher was amazing. The night before Elsa had simply—or not so simply—manoeuvred it so it was lying on top of the air mattress. At dawn, as the team above prepared the gear to lift him, she used its pump to inflate the sides. The air-filled bumpers would protect him as it was hauled to the surface.

It had head, neck and spine support. It had full body, pressure-point-free immobilisation. It had cross fix restraints and ten carry handles.

'It's also X-ray-transparent and it'll carry anyone up to two hundred and fifty kilograms,' Elsa told him proudly, as she adjusted the straps that held him fixed. 'Though if you'd weighed that much we might have had to raise a small army to haul you up.'

He didn't smile. He was now totally immobilised and he'd never felt so helpless.

Above ground the team was fixing cabling from one side of the unsafe ground to the other. What that meant was that team members could safely fix anchors above the hole, then abseil down if needed, or have someone stay safely above ground to guide him up.

Elsa was explaining things as she worked. She was upping his drug dose as well.

'It's a great stretcher and we're a good team,' she told him. 'But we can't stop it being bumpy while we carry you down the mountain. I'm sorry, Marc, but there'll need to be a bit of biting the bullet on your part.'

'You guys are saving me. I won't be whinging.'

That brought a wry smile.

'What, you don't believe me?'

'We'll see,' she said enigmatically. 'We hauled a tourist up a cliff face a few weeks back. He'd been trying to take a selfie, climbed the safety rail to get a better angle and leaned out a little too far over a fifty-foot drop to the sea below. He was super lucky to be caught on a ledge fifteen feet down, with only a fractured arm and bruises. It took our guys hours to pull him up, but do you think he was grateful? The first thing he did was abuse us because we hadn't brought up his camera. He shouted at us practically the

whole time before we managed to get him air-
lifted out of here. The fact that his camera had
fallen the whole way down and the team would
have been risking their own lives to get it simply
didn't register.'

'People do stupid things,' he managed, cha-
grined that he was in the same category.

'They do, and you did, but at least you've been
grateful,' she told him, smiling down at him.
'Speaking of which, I've been thinking of that
St Moritz offer. I should say no and leave it at
that, but if you're serious…'

'I am.'

'Then could we swap St Moritz for a reclin-
ing lift chair for our nursing home patients?' she
asked tentatively. 'Or maybe even two if you're
feeling super generous. We have a couple of oldies who can't get out of chairs without help, and
it makes them feel so dependent.'

'I know how that feels,' he said grimly, feeling
the straps holding him immobile.

'Then it's a great time to ask,' she said, and
grinned again. 'Damn, I didn't bring a pen and
paper or I'd have you sign a promissory note—
before we bring you to the surface and you get
all St Moritzy again.'

'I won't get… St Moritzy. I've said goodbye
to that fantasy.'

'You'll be back there next year,' she told him. 'While we enjoy two great lift chairs.'

'You won't enjoy two lift chairs.'

'You want to bet? Seeing Marigold Peterson get up from her chair and walk out to the veranda without having to wait for a nurse to help her... You take your St Moritz, Dr Pierce. I'll take Marigold's pleasure any day.'

He looked at her curiously, this competent, brisk young woman. With the dawn had come natural light, filtering down and angled so he could see her. The night before she'd been a shadow behind the lantern, or maybe he'd been too hazy, drug affected to see her clearly. Now he had a proper look.

She looked competent. Determined. Her jeans and windcheater were filthy, her hair dust-caked, but he could see more than just a general impression. She was only little, a package of efficiency about five feet two or three. Slight. Wiry? He'd have to say that—there was no trace of an idle life or an indulged lifestyle about her. Her hair seemed almost flame-red beneath the dust. It looked as if it could be amazing but right now her curls were tied back in a practical, business-like ponytail.

Watching her as she adjusted his straps, he had a sudden irrational urge to reach out and release the ponytail. He wanted to see what those curls looked like floating free.

Yeah, like that was a good idea. Patient hitting on doctor? She was leaving the lower part of his good arm free—so he could scratch his nose if he wanted—but looking at that determined chin, feeling the brisk competence she was exuding, he thought she'd have his arms tied down in an instant if he tried it on.

He had the very strong impression that Dr Elsa McCrae was not a woman to mess with.

And she had principles. She'd just knocked back what to her, he suspected, might be the holiday of a lifetime, in order to barter for two chairs for her oldies. He'd seen the flash of amazement in her eyes as he'd made his offer. He'd also seen regret slam home. Common sense had taken over. With this woman, it probably always would.

'You like family medicine?' he asked curiously, watching her face as she worked.

'I like making people feel better.'

'Then you've made me feel better,' he said—and to his astonishment he saw a hint of a blush.

But she brushed it away, got efficient again fast. 'Then I've done my job,' she said lightly. 'Now…you want to say goodbye to your nice cosy bedroom before we hoist you up?'

'I thought I was going to die in this nice cosy bedroom. I hate this nice cosy bedroom.'

'Then let's get you out of here,' she said and glanced up. 'Righto, people, haul him up.'

She'd say this for him, the guy was stoic.

The trip down the mountain was tough on the carriers, but it'd be a whole lot tougher for the man on the stretcher. The path was rough, crisscrossed by tree roots. They were forced to detour round boulders the path makers had been unable to shift. With the dawn, five more of the islanders had come up to help, so there were two shifts of four to carry him down, but Marc had to endure the journey as best he could.

Elsa followed behind. She wasn't permitted to be a stretcher bearer.

'You slip and who do you think'll patch you up?' Macka had growled.

'Grandpa?'

'Yeah, and then he'd have this fella in one bed and you in another, and all the Christmas tourist influx to cope with on his own. You were a damned fool to go down that hole by yourself, Doc. We won't have you taking any more risks now.'

So she walked behind, watching her step, chatting to the guys on the alternate bearer shift, watching the man on the stretcher.

He was hurting—she could see that, but there was little she could do about it. She had his leg and arm firmly fixed but there was no way to stop the stretcher being jolted.

He'd said he wouldn't complain, and he didn't, but she could see the tension on his face.

And the mortification.

He was a cardiologist, a city surgeon. These guys were top of the tree in the medical profession. He'd offered her a holiday in St Moritz without blinking, and she'd heard in his voice that he was serious. He'd be earning big money. Huge.

He looked—what? Mid-thirties? He was lean, dark-haired, tanned beneath the dust. Even now, strapped to the stretcher and in pain, she could see an air of authority about him.

He was a guy who was used to being in charge of his world.

He wasn't in charge now. He was totally at the mercy of the people carrying his stretcher. Macka, a burly sixty-something policeman. Denise, the island mechanic, also in her sixties. Little, round, always grease-stained, she was the best square dancer on the island, tough as old boots. Graham, the local accountant, fiftyish, who wore prim three-piece suits for five days a week but as soon as he was out of the office he donned tartan lumberjack gear. Mike, a still pimply kid who'd just finished his schooling and would be off to university in the autumn, but who spent all his spare time climbing and abseiling.

The alternate shift consisted of just as motley a collection of characters, but every one of them was competent. They knew this island. They knew what they were doing.

Marc was forced to lie on his stretcher and trust them.

Elsa had once asked if she could have a go at being carried on the stretcher, just to see what it felt like. They'd strapped her down and taken her over a rough path and she'd felt almost claustrophobic, totally at the mercy of a team who could drop her at any minute. They wouldn't. She knew them and trusted them inherently, but Marc would have no such trust.

She watched his face and saw the strain and knew instinctively that this guy's life was all about control.

'Pain level?' she asked, coming alongside the stretcher. 'You want a top-up?'

'I'm fuzzy as it is,' he told her. 'I want my wits about me.'

'So if we drop you, you might be able to save yourself? It won't happen,' she told him. 'This team has never dropped a punter yet.'

He grunted and went back to staring straight upward. She fell back again and continued to watch him closely.

His control looked as if it was stretched to the limit. He didn't complain though. Not a whinge.

'He's a doctor, you say,' Macka said to her at the next change of shift.

'Yep.'

'You reckon we could organise a plane strike or something so we can set his leg and put him behind your grandpa's clinic desk for a week or six? Give your grandpa—and you—a bit of a break?'

'As if,' she said and then looked curiously up at Macka. 'Why do you say that?'

'It's only…well, I dropped in to pick up supplies before we came up to find you,' he told her. 'And I thought old Doc was looking a bit grey around the edges.'

'He's probably just worried about me.'

'Aye, that'd be it,' Macka said, but he sounded doubtful and Elsa winced and thought, *No, please, Grandpa, don't get sick.*

He had renal problems. He had heart problems.

He'd promised her he'd live for ever, and as a kid she'd depended on that promise. Now…not so much and the thought made her feel ill.

Her attention distracted, she stumbled on a tree root and Macka caught her arm and steadied her.

'Thanks,' she muttered to Macka, and then to herself she said, *Cut it out, focus on now.*

Finally they were down. Macka's police-van-cum-ambulance was parked near the start of the walking track. Elsa left them loading their pa-

tient on board and took her own car—and Sherlock—back to the hospital. Grandpa came out to
greet her, and she had the opportunity to check
him out as he bent to pat the exuberant Sherlock.

He did look tired, she conceded. Grey? Maybe.
Robert McCrae had been the island's doctor for
fifty years and he hated slowing down, but she
was going to have to insist.

Though where did that leave her? When Robert
had started here, the population of the island had
been three hundred with practically no outsid-
ers. Now it was a tourist mecca, its population of
seven hundred exploding over the mainland holiday breaks. The outer islands had tourists flood-
ing them too, and she and Robert were still the
only doctors.

It wouldn't matter so much if tourists didn't
insist on doing such risky things. Like Marcus
Pierce, trekking up an unknown mountain trail
by himself and letting no one know where he
was going. If Sherlock hadn't found him… She
closed her eyes, unable to bear thinking of the
consequences.

But he'd be thinking of the consequences, she
thought. He'd have spent over twenty-four hours
thinking the absolute worst. He'd probably need
trauma counselling if he wasn't to cop PTSD. She
needed a trauma counsellor on staff.

The trauma counsellor would have to be her.

But for now she was late for morning clinic and Grandpa looked as if he needed a good lie-down—he'd also have spent a wakeful night worrying about her. And then there was Christmas! Without turkeys? Even as she got out of the car she saw the hospital cook flapping in the background, waiting to talk to her. Waiting for Elsa to solve the turkey problem.

First things first. A shower. She felt disgusting and she guessed she smelled disgusting too. She had to move on, and she needed help. 'Grandpa, you know the situation?' she asked him. 'This guy needs fluids, intravenous antibiotics—he has a couple of decent lacerations—a bed bath to get most of the grime off before we can touch him. What's the situation with evacuation to the mainland?'

'Not possible,' Robert told her. 'There's sti smoke haze drifting our way. Unless it's life death we're on our own.'

'Then we ultrasound his shoulder and X his leg and hope it's fixable here.' She grim 'You know he's a doctor?'

'The worst kind of patient.'

'You'd know,' she said and managed 'Like me giving you orders to get eigh sleep no matter what? I'm betting you di much last night.'

'I can sleep when I'm dead,' Robe

ply. 'Not when there's work to do. Go on and get yourself clean, girl, and worry about them who need it.'

The woman who appeared at his bedside an hour later stunned him.

In the gloom of the cave, layered in dust, wearing hiking gear, he'd thought she was good-looking.

Now though…she pushed back the curtain of the examination cubicle and he had to blink.

She was dressed in sky-blue trousers and a soft white shirt, both almost concealed by a white coat. Her shoes were sensible flats, but they were bright pink and she'd tied her hair back in a matching pink ribbon. The pink should clash with her hair, but it certainly didn't. She wore little if any make-up, but she didn't need it. She didn't need anything. With her flaming curls, her sparkling green eyes, the flash of colour in her clothing…she was enough to make a man feel better all on her own.

And he'd been feeling better anyway, soaking in the luxury of a decent mattress, pillows, warmth, no more bumping stretcher and enough painkiller to make him dozy.

'I think I've died and gone to heaven,' he managed. She smiled—and that made things even more confusing. It was a killer of a smile. A smile that made a man…

Get a grip. He needed to. It must be the drugs that were making him feel…woozy?

'Feeling better, then?' she asked.

'You'd better believe it. Did you ask for only two lift chairs? Try asking for a hundred. Half my kingdom if you like.'

'I'll believe it when I see it,' she said with a smile that robbed her words of offence. 'You have no idea of how many rescued tourists who've left the island promising largesse, never to be heard of again.'

'I keep my promises,' he told her, and her smile slipped. She looked at him for a long moment and then gave a determined little nod.

'I believe you will,' she said. 'Thank you. But mind, we won't hold you to it. Do nothing until you're well, and then think about it. I had no business to ask.'

'As I had no business to expect you to save my life.'

'It's what we do,' she told him. 'Our whole team, including Sherlock. Do you need to let your people know what's happening?'

'One of the nurses lent me a phone.'

'And you got through? Great. I guess no one will be able to rush to your side before the mainland smoke clears, but I hope you stopped them being anxious. Tell them they can ring me if they want reassurance.'

He thought of Kayla's reaction to his call. Admittedly, he hadn't told her about being trapped—he'd just said he'd fallen while scattering his mother's ashes—but even so she'd been less than sympathetic. She'd asked incisive questions about his injuries but once she was reassured about their severity she'd moved on.

She'd go to St Moritz anyway, she'd decided. She'd let their friends know their party would be one person short, but she was busy. She had to pack. There'd been brief words of commiseration before she disconnected, and that was that.

'No one wants reassurance,' he said brusquely, and Elsa gave him a searching look and then flicked the overhead screen to blank, so it showed only white light.

'Okay, then. You want to see your X-rays? They're reassuring at least.'

'They're only reassuring if they show no break at all.'

'You still dreaming of St Moritz? Move on,' she told him and put up the X-ray.

It showed a clean break of both tibia and fibula. Slight dislocation but no splintering. It could have been much, much worse.

'I can set this,' she told him. 'Grandpa and I concur. We'd rather send you to the mainland to a decent orthopod, but you know the restrictions on flights at the moment. I did specific training for remote medicine, including orthopaedics, before

I came here, and so did Grandpa. We've both set breaks like this, and so far we haven't managed to put a single foot on backwards. Grandpa's competent with anaesthetics and I'll do the setting. The alternative is to leave it as it is until evacuation, but even with strong splinting we both know movement's possible. Which means circulation could be blocked. So I'm asking you to trust us.'

'I trust you.'

She gave another of her brisk nods, a gesture he was starting to know. And like.

'The good news is that your ultrasound shows little damage to your shoulder. No tears. It'll be sore for a while and you'll have to protect it, but you seem to have done no long-term damage.'

'Your grandfather told me that.'

'Right, then,' she said. 'You've had nothing to eat since your muesli bars before we started the trek. We'll wait another couple of hours to make sure they're well down, and then we'll set your leg. Meanwhile, I have a clinic queue a mile long so you won't see me until Theatre. The nurses will look after you.'

'They already have.' He looked into her face and behind the smile, behind the briskness, he saw strain. She would have slept badly last night, if at all. He knew enough of this woman to accept that her first responsibility would have been to check on him, probably hourly, so she wouldn't have let herself fall into a deep sleep.

'You've had quite a night yourself. Your grandpa can't run clinic while you have a rest?'

'I wish,' she said wryly. She was up-to-date with the clinic news now. 'Grandpa was up during the night himself, with a fisherman who decided at midnight that his finger was infected. He hurt it last week. It was only when his wife thought sweating in bed was a problem that they decided to call for help. So it's Grandpa who needs the rest, not that he'll take it.'

'I wish I could help.'

'You can, by being sensible and compliant and not throwing out a single complication,' she told him. 'Focus, Dr Pierce. I want an exemplary patient.'

'I'll do my best.'

'And I'll do mine,' she told him. 'Now, you rest for all of us. See you in Theatre.'

And she was gone, her white coat a blur as she closed the door behind her.

He was left with the impression of capability and practicality. And more. An indefinable something.

He'd made a lot more work for this woman. She should be angry with him. She was just resigned, he thought. And capable and practical.

And that indefinable...something.

CHAPTER SIX

IN THE END Marc's surgery was straightforward. Her grandfather gave the general anaesthetic—this was the way they normally worked, and it worked well now. The leg was relatively easy to stabilise. She cleaned and debrided lacerations, put in stitches to the deepest and put a back slab on his leg. It'd eventually be a full cast, but not until the stitches were out and the swelling had gone down.

Despite the reassurance of the ultrasound, she still wanted to test shoulder rotation without the pain caused by the bruising. She found nothing to disturb her.

He'd got off lightly, Elsa thought as she left him in the care of the theatre staff.

Next.

Somehow she convinced Robert to take a nap—which was a worry all on its own. Yes, he'd had to work during the night but both of them were accustomed to doing that. Her grandfather hated conceding weakness, and his agreement to have an afternoon sleep surprised her. Now, not only did she have a queue a mile long at her clinic, she had the niggling fear that he wasn't telling all.

'Maybe I'm coming down with a cold,' he muttered when she pressed him. 'Or maybe it's just worrying about you, girl. Tell you what, you stop worrying about me and I'll stop worrying about you. Which means quitting with the diving down unknown caves.'

She grinned and asked no more questions, but as she sat in clinic and saw patient after patient, her sense of unease deepened.

And clinic was made worse by the fact that every patient wanted to discuss her night's adventures.

'They say he's a doctor. Louise Pierce's boy.' Marc's mother had been a member of the local climbing group, sometimes spending so much time here the islanders considered her almost one of them. 'Why didn't he take one of us up to the peak with him? Damned idiot, he could have killed you too.'

'No fear of that,' she told them. 'I had Sherlock and he has a nose for holes. He does the hunting. I stick to paths.'

'Except when you're rescuing tourists. What does he think he's doing, putting *our* doc at risk?'

And there was the nub, Elsa thought wearily as the day wore on. She was *their* doctor. She knew the islanders were fond of her, but they also depended on her.

She fielded a call from Tony, who put it more than bluntly. 'You had no right to put yourself at risk, Elsa. Don't you know what's at stake?'

'The whole island needs me. Yes, I know.'

'I need you.'

'No more than any other islander,' she said, trying to keep irritation out of her voice. One unwise date and he practically had her wedded, bedded and mother to half a dozen little Tonys. 'Tony, leave it. You know I had no choice.'

'If he's fool enough to have fallen…'

'I should have left him there, cold and hurting? I don't think so. Sorry, Tony, I need to run.'

'I want to see you. How about dinner?'

'No chance,' she said and cut him short. It was getting to the stage where hints weren't enough. 'Tony, stop it with the idea that we're a couple. We're not.'

And she did need to run. It was already Thursday. Christmas Day was Sunday and how on earth was she going to get everything done by then? Dinner was a sandwich grabbed from the kitchen fridge, eaten while she typed up patient notes for the day with her spare hand—who knew that a five-fingered typist could be so efficient? Finally she headed over to the wards to check all was well before she could—hopefully—get some sleep.

She found Marc propped up on pillows, his leg in traction, scowling at a laptop. Actually…not a laptop. She recognised it as a generic tablet usually kept in the kids' ward.

'What, is Dorothy Dinosaur not co-operating?' she asked, smiling at the sight of one gorgeous guy, sparsely dressed in a white hospital gown, holding a pink, sparkly, dinosaur-decorated tablet.

He didn't smile back.

'One of your nurses kindly unlocked it from kid-safe mode,' he muttered, still glowering. 'So I managed to download my files from the ether and I'm trying to get some work done. But every time I try to save anything, it defaults back to Dorothy and locks me down. And the nurse won't give me the password. She comes in when she has time and unlocks it again like she's doing me a huge favour.'

She grinned at that. 'Maggie's old school,' she told him. 'She likes discipline in her hospital, and to her everyone under the age of forty is a kid.' She tugged up a chair, sat and took the tablet from him and typed in the password. 'There you go.'

'You're not going to give me the password either?'

'I'm with Maggie. We have two small boys

in the kids' ward right now who'd barter their mother for the password. Who's to say you won't sell it on? Plus Maggie's knitting patterns are on this tablet.' She relented. 'You know you should be sleeping. Your body will demand sleep, even if your mind hasn't caught up yet. But I can lend you my spare laptop if you want. The med stuff is locked but I'll trust you not to try and break in.'

'Gee, thanks.'

'You're welcome.' She looked curiously at him. 'So you really came all this way without so much as a change of socks?'

'It was supposed to be a back and forth in a day trip,' he said, sighing and setting the tablet aside. 'Before she died, Mum told me it'd take three hours max to climb to the peak. The plane arrived at nine and was leaving at six, so getting here and back in a day seemed easy. I had a research paper to assess on the flight—a printout that's still sitting in a locker at the airport—so I didn't need my laptop. I can do urgent stuff on my phone, but that's now smashed.'

'So you're screenless.' She shook her head. 'That's truly horrible. But moving on…apart from your lack of screen, tell me what hurts?'

'Just about everything,' he admitted. 'But mostly my pride.' He pushed himself further up in the bed, grimacing with pain. He looked ruffled, she thought, and also…strangely defenceless? He was a big man, tall, lean, muscular. The dirt he'd been covered with was gone and he'd shaved, but his dark, wavy hair was ruffled as if he'd been raking it in frustration. Despite his immobilised leg, his arm in a sling and his loose hospital gown, his strongly boned face and what she could see of his ripped body combined to give the impression of barely contained strength. He looked powerful but confined, edgy to be gone.

His pride was hurting? Yeah, she could see it. For such a man to be in this position...

'I can't do much about your pride,' she told him, 'but I can do something about the aches and pain.'

'I'll make do with paracetamol.'

She grinned and motioned back to the tablet, where Dorothy and her dinosaurs were circling the perimeter of Marc's word document. 'I guess if you want to do battle with Dorothy you need to keep your wits about you, and the stronger pain-killers might indeed make you feel a bit fuzzy,' she admitted. 'But there's no prizes for heroics, Dr Pierce. Your leg's a mass of bruises and lacerations, to say nothing of the break. Your shoulder must be giving you heaps. Plus your back... You can't see, but it's spectacularly black and blue.' Her voice grew serious. 'You were incredibly lucky not to break your spine.'

'I was incredibly lucky in more ways than one,'

he said, and almost involuntarily he reached out with his good arm and took her hand in his. And held it tightly, as if reassuring himself she was real. 'I was lucky because of one Dr Elsa Mc-Crae,' he said softly. 'Elsa, I'll never forget it.'

She stilled, looked down at their linked hands. It had been a casual gesture, an impulse, but their hands stayed locked.

She'd spent a long, scary night with this man. He must have been terrified when she'd found him, but he hadn't let on. He'd been matter-of-fact, uncomplaining, holding it together.

He was grateful. It was the only reason he was holding her hand.

Or maybe it was more than that. Maybe the terrors were still with him. Maybe he needed the contact.

She told herself that as she let her hand stay where it was. She'd had a hard night too. The work was piling up around her, but for just a moment she let herself be held. She felt the strength and comfort of his grip. She even let herself believe she wasn't alone.

But she was alone, and there was work a mile high to be waded through. She needed to get on.

She should tug her hand away.

But still she didn't. For his sake, she told herself. Not for hers.

'It'll be a darn sight easier to forget gratitude—

forget anything else that's bothering you—if you let me give you some decent painkillers,' she managed, and was annoyed to find that her voice was unsteady. 'Have some now and I'll write you up more for the night. Just ask Maggie, she's on all night.'

'Maggie's scary,' he said, and she grinned.

'Better men than you are scared of Maggie. Wielding a bedpan, she's a force to be reckoned with, but she's a fine nurse.' Finally, reluctantly, she tugged back her hand and rose. Was it her imagination or had there been reluctance on his part to let her go? It was understandable, she told herself. He'd need human contact after feeling such fear.

And her reaction?

This was ridiculous. Moving on…

'Is…is there anything else you need?'

'A set of clean clothes?' he ventured, back to being practical. 'You cut off my pants. At least I didn't lose my wallet so I hope I can purchase something to wear.'

'I'd like to keep you in for a couple of days,' she warned him. 'I'm still worried about clots.'

'That's two of us,' he said grimly. 'I know the risks. So clothes can wait but I'd kill for decent pyjamas. Even more for a phone.'

'I can help there as well. Didn't you already use our ward phone? It has overseas capability—we cope with a lot of tourists and you'd be astonished at how many of them lose their phones. I'll tell Maggie to drop it in again.'

'I'd like my own,' he growled. Without his phone he felt stranded. Or even more stranded than he already was. 'Is there anyone on the island who could organise me one?'

'Jason,' she told him. 'He's a cray fisherman but he does a nice little sideline in technology. His boat's due in tonight so I'll ask him to come and see you tomorrow. Anything's possible if you're prepared to pay. In the meantime, Maggie will bring you my laptop. We'll even unlock the passwords for you.'

'Thank you,' he said stiffly, and she thought this was a guy who hated being out of control. Not having his phone, not having the internet would be killing him. But his next question surprised her. 'What about you? Are you going to bed now?'

'Soon,' she lied.

'Soon, as in after you've seen what…another ten patients?'

'Only one,' she admitted and then decided maybe she needed to talk to this guy as a colleague. For some reason he had her unsettled and she couldn't figure it out. 'Mathew Hobson rang fifteen minutes ago and thinks he might have been bitten by a redback spider,' she told him.

'He's on his way in. He'll be fine, though. He met one once and never got over it—now every time he feels a prick from an ant or mosquito he thinks the worst.' She glanced at her watch. 'He should be arriving any minute.'

'And then you'll get to bed?'

'In time. I have the thirty-odd Christmas gifts to wrap over the next couple of days, and I'm already way behind.'

'Thirty!'

She smiled and shrugged. She should leave— she didn't have time to stay and gossip with patients—but those dark eyes of his were watching her with a hint of warmth, of humour, of understanding. He *was* a colleague, she thought. A real medical colleague who understood the pressure she was under.

Like a friend.

Whatever, the need to tell him was suddenly overwhelming.

'I do a thing,' she told him. 'On Christmas Day.'

'A thing?'

'Well, it's not all me,' she told him. 'But the gifts are me. I'm not sure what you know about this island.'

'Not much.'

'Yeah, well, it's been a quiet little backwater for years. We don't have decent educational facilities here—the kids have to go away for school if they want to do more than fish or farm. We now have a big tourist network, but local kids don't see that as an opportunity. Most of our local kids leave when they're old enough. Some come back but most don't. That means we're left with an ageing population and at Christmas a lot of lonely oldies.'

'Which is where you come in?'

'A lot of us come in,' she told him. 'The year I came back to the island I copped literally scores of calls on Christmas Day from oldies who really did feel ill. There's nothing like loneliness to make a slight niggle seem like something frightening. Then the next year Jonas Cruikshank, a local farmer, committed suicide on Christmas Day. His wife had died six months earlier, neither of his kids could make it back to the island and it must have been all too much for him.' She shrugged awkwardly. 'The local church ladies had put on a welfare-type dinner, but he hadn't put his name down for it. Why would he? Come and admit that he was one of the lonely? He had far too much pride. His death hit us all dreadfully, so after that we decided to change things up a bit. Make Christmas fun.'

'You mean *you* decided to make it fun.'

'I did,' she said a trifle defensively.

'How?'

What was she doing, sitting talking when she

had so much to do? This guy was a patient. She'd written him up for the drugs he'd need for the night—if he'd take them. Her work here was done.

But this was Christmas.

Jonas Cruikshank had been a friend more than a patient. His wife had babysat her as a little girl. Jonas had given her her first dog, the predecessor of a long line leading to Sherlock. His death had cast a pall over the whole island, and the next year she'd overridden all objections and done it her way.

And this guy had asked. He should be sleeping but he seemed wide awake and she wouldn't mind…just talking for a little while.

She shut her eyes for a moment, closing her mind to the to-do list still waiting for her. She tugged her chair back up to the bed and sat. And talked.

'For a start, I moved our communal Christmas dinner out of the church hall,' she told him.

'You're not religious?'

'I didn't say that. The churches on this island do a fabulous job, but the only one with a hall big enough to take us has walls covered in Easter images. They're beautiful but they're sad. I want fun at my Christmas celebration, Dr Pierce, not suffering. So I moved the whole thing to the footy ground training room. It's huge.'

'So let me guess,' he said, bemused. 'You now have portraits of sweaty, post grand final football teams, and rolls of past players?'

'They take 'em down for us,' she said smugly. 'They didn't want to, but three years back the whole team came down with norovirus two days before playing the grand final with one of the neighbouring islands. You have no idea how hard Grandpa and I worked to rehydrate those guys, and in the end we got them all match fit and they won. So the coach's speech included a public declaration that the footy club stood in our debt. Same as you. You're donating lift chairs, or I hope you are. They've donated a testosterone-free training room every Christmas, they take down their pictures and honour rolls and they even throw in a decorated tree for good measure.'

Marc chuckled. She met his eyes and saw a twinkle lurking in their depths. She chuckled too, and all at once she felt better. As if the weariness had lifted a little.

She should go now, she told herself.

She didn't.

'So you have a hall,' he prompted, sounding fascinated. 'What else?'

'I pull in favours wherever I can find 'em,' she told him. 'I also now have Douglas McCurdie's puddings, and that's really something.'

'Puddings?'

'Douglas is a local poultry farmer. His wife used to make a Christmas pudding which was a legend among her family, and when she died he found the recipe and started making them to sell. They're awesome but he's canny—he sells them for a ridiculous amount through a trendy Sydney outlet. But he was friends with Jonas, and when I twisted his arm he agreed to provide them—as long as he's on the guest list. He's lonely and it's a pride saver for him, too. And so it's spiralled. We have some of the best island cooks competing to have their food accepted. Grandpa and I have people we decree need to be invited, but the rest of the places are up for ballot, and that list's a mile long. But if you volunteer to help you become part of it. It's fabulous.'

'And the gifts?' he said cautiously, sounding entranced.

'They're just for the specials. If I did gifts for everyone I'd go nuts. But the islanders who don't have anyone waiting at home, or those too ill or elderly to have a decent Christmas themselves—they get a gift, and those gifts are personal. No handkerchiefs and socks from me.'

'Like what?'

'Little things,' she told him. 'You've already figured money on this island is tight so they can't be big. But I have spies in the welfare shop, with the fishermen, with the local tradies, with whoever I can think of to help, and I have a plan that lasts all year.'

He'd forgotten the pain in his leg. The pain all over his body. She had him fascinated.

'So tell me about your plan.'

'Well…like geraniums for Sandra Carter,' she told him. 'Sandra's been alone since her husband and her son drowned in a boating accident six years back. But she adores geraniums—she reckons she has every variety known to man. Six months ago we had an evacuation flight arrive without its usual doctor. They'd expected a routine problem, but it turned nasty so I had to go with them to Sydney. I needed to stay overnight and took a dusk walk and saw the most amazing geranium—I swear it was almost black. I knocked on the door and the lady gave me a cutting and it's actually grown. I reckon Sandra will be beside herself when she sees it. Not all my things hit the sweet spot, but I do my best. I have a "Beware, Vicious Dog" sign for May Trent with her ancient chihuahua. I have a perfect nautilus shell for Louise Addington whose grandson broke hers when he was here last holiday. I have a second-hand book on making artificial flies for Ron Nesbit—he spends his life fly-fishing. Oh, and I had another triumph—I found an ancient pottery wheel for Gay Ryan, who's always wanted to try throwing pots, and it goes with a promise of lessons from Chris Baker, who's an excellent local potter. That took me taking Chris's kid's appendix out to wheedle. So many things—and they all have to be wrapped.'

'Including the pottery wheel?' he said faintly.

'I'll use a long piece of string for that,' she told him. 'It'll lead to the janitor's room, where the wheel will be set up. I'll wrap a box with the end of the string in it to give to Gay. The trick is to make every gift look ordinary. It's become a bit of a thing—the islanders love it. I have people suggesting stuff now, but no one knows until Christmas Day what the gifts are. Actually, that's not true. Grandpa knows because he helps—he loves it too.' She paused and bit her lip. 'Or mostly he does. He's not even asking about it this year.'

And that was enough to haul her out of her story, to make her remember reality. 'Sorry,' she said contritely. 'That's far too much information about my hobby horse. You need to rest.'

'So do you.'

'I don't have a black and blue body. I'll send Maggie in with something.'

'You're worried about your grandpa?'

'Doesn't everyone worry about their grandpa? He should be...' She paused and managed a smile and shrugged. 'No. I was going to say he should be retired, but sitting in a rocker watching the world go by isn't his scene. He'll die in the traces.

Except I don't want it to be…well, not for a very long time yet.'

This was personal. What was she doing, talking personal with a patient? Marc was watching her face—reading her astutely? The thought was unsettling.

If he was unsettling her then all the more reason for her to leave, but she didn't, and it was Marc who spoke up next.

'How sick is he?'

She sighed and spread her hands. Why not? She'd come this far. 'His renal problems aren't bad enough for dialysis or transplant yet, but they're worrying,' she told him. 'Plus there's his heart. He had a minor attack last year. We had to fly him to Sydney, where they put in a stent and gave him orders to slow down. Which he refuses to do. He should have gone back last month for a check-up but of course he won't. And don't you dare tell him I told you.'

'I won't. But you know I'm a cardiologist. Maybe I…'

'Could examine him before you leave? I'd like to see you try—I can only imagine what he'd say if he thought I was worrying a patient on his behalf.'

'I'm a colleague.'

'Says the man with his leg in plaster, an arm in a sling and bruises all over him.' She forced a smile back onto her face and decided she really did need to go now. The fact that this man was looking at her with empathy, with understanding, with concern…

She didn't need any of it. She didn't!

'Let me help you wrap your parcels,' he said, and she blinked.

'What, you?'

'That's hardly a gracious response.' He was sitting up in bed, smiling at her, and she thought he was bruised and battered, he was wearing a generic hospital gown and the man had no business to look as sexy as he did. Or have a smile that twisted something inside her that had no business being twisted.

'My arm's sore,' he told her, watching her with eyes that seemed to see far too much. 'But it's not terrible. My leg will stop me hiking for a while but neither of them preclude me from being useful. My friends have gone to St Moritz without me, and I'm at a loose end. So how about loading me up with lists, gifts, wrapping paper and sticky tape? My wrapping might be a bit off, but I can cover things.'

'I can't…'

'Ask me? You weren't forward in asking for lift chairs.'

'That's different. That's for the hospital.'

'And this is personal? I don't think so.'

'But it is,' she said seriously. 'If you knew the pleasure those gifts give me…'

'Because they're for other people,' he said gently. 'Who gives you a gift, Dr McCrae?'

'If you saw the selection of chocolates out at Reception…'

'I'm not talking of chocolates.'

'They're more appropriate than an offer to fly me to St Moritz,' she flung at him and then flushed. 'No. Sorry, I'm very grateful.'

'You shouldn't feel grateful.'

'I don't, because I have all the gifts I need.' He'd been watching her, their gazes almost locked, but now she deliberately lowered her eyes, staring blindly towards the chart at the end of the bed. 'I…if you really do mean it…about the wrapping…'

'I really do mean it.'

'Then I may well take you up on it,' she told him, still not looking at him. 'You might still be running on adrenalin now, but I suspect you'll find you need to sleep tomorrow. Even if you don't think it, your injuries will take their toll. But if you're still here on Saturday… Maybe I could put a quarantine sign on your door and tell the nurses you're desperate for rest. A couple of them will be suspicious, but it'll give you privacy.'

'I'd barricade the door with my bed tray,' he

told her solemnly. 'Secrets R Us. Speaking of which…'

'Marc, I really do need to go.' She did, too. This guy was making her feel more and more unsettled.

'Yeah, but I have a favour to ask,' he told her. 'My clothes are torn, filthy and bloodstained. And this gown…'

'It's a very nice gown,' she said and managed to smile. His gaze had met hers again and the twinkle in those dark eyes…

She had to get out of here!

'It's a great gown as far as gowns go,' he told her, the twinkle intensifying. 'But as far as secrets go… Every time I get out of bed I need to clutch my modesty around me and hope.'

'There's nothing under there the nurses haven't seen a hundred times before.'

'Dr McCrae…'

'Yes… Dr Pierce?'

'Could you please, please, please, see if you can find me some clothes. Some decent pyjamas.'

'I'm already on it,' she told him. 'Kylie—she's the lass who delivers your meals—has a sister who works in the charity store. I've sent her home with a list.'

'The welfare store!'

'There's not a great range on the island,' she told him. 'Mostly we buy online. It takes about a month to get here, but if you're prepared to wait…'

'So it's the welfare store or nothing.' He sounded revolted and she chuckled.

'You never know. I saw Brenda Larsen drop off her husband's purple pyjamas only last week. Linus has gone up a size, from enormous to eye-popping. They're a bit stretched across the tummy but otherwise in perfect condition. If you're lucky they might still be there.'

'Elsa…'

She chuckled and threw up her hands. 'I know, every sense is offended. I'll send Maggie in with laptop, phone and drugs but you do need to sleep. I'm going.'

'Before I toss a pillow at you.'

'I'm gone,' she said, and was out of there, tugging the door firmly closed behind her.

He lay and stared at the closed door for a long time.

Maggie didn't bring the laptop or the phone or the drugs. She would soon, he thought. He'd shown her he'd been irritated, and she'd be making her point. Nurses were a bad breed to get off-side. He knew that. As a cardiovascular surgeon he couldn't get by without the help of his extraordinary team, and he made a point of ensuring they weren't stressed.

Maggie had been busy, and he'd pushed her too hard to try and get the tablet password reset.

Was the password so important? Elsa had said there were two little boys in the kids' ward. Did he know what was wrong with them? Did he know how busy the nursing staff were?

He was getting the feeling he knew how busy Elsa was. Too damned busy. Plus she was tired.

Because she'd climbed down into unchartered territory to save him. She'd spent what must have been an almost sleepless night. She'd accompanied him back down the mountain this morning and then operated on his leg.

She had a grandpa with a bad heart, and a community dependent on her as its only full-time doctor.

And he'd been making a fuss about a password.

Because his work was so much more important?

He thought suddenly back to medical school, to the first of the numerous sessions where specialists outlined their roles, where students were expected to think seriously about which path they'd take.

The cardiovascular surgeon had been impressive. He remembered the talk clearly. 'We're at the cutting edge of technology, saving lives which even ten years ago would have been lost. We demand the highest level of intellectual and physical skill. I believe it's the peak of medical expertise—exciting, challenging and, yes, immensely lucrative. Only the best of you need think of applying and only the best of the best will make the grade.'

That was for him, he'd thought. Studying was a breeze. Cutting edge surgery excited him. As for lucrative…who didn't want lucrative? With the wealth he'd inherited from his parents he hardly needed it, but still…

But Elsa…

He thought back to that same lecture, the small, greying man who'd represented family doctors.

'We're not cutting edge,' he'd said quietly. 'In most cases I confess we're not all that lucrative, although most of us make a respectable living. But we do save lives. Not as dramatically as my compatriots on this panel, no life-saving heart or brain surgery for us. But we find and refer, and along the way we pick up the pieces of people's lives and we do our best to patch them together. We try to stop the dramas before they start. Most of us have a community we care for deeply, and we'll do anything for them. A mum with post-natal depression…a coal miner with a cough he thinks is nothing…that's who we're here for and it gives us just as much satisfaction as our more esteemed peers.'

Marc had hardly listened.

His father had been a neurologist. His mother had been a brilliant medical researcher. He was expected to be bright, and bright young doctors followed bright young professions.

They never saw mums with postnatal depression. They never saw a guy with a cold and pushed him to have a chest X-ray.

They never sat up late on the nights before Christmas and wrapped twenty or thirty parcels for needy locals.

He thought of his mother, who'd said she'd loved this island. Maybe she had, but she'd only come here to climb. She'd never have wrapped thirty gifts for people she hardly knew.

She'd been as selfish as he was.

Selfish? The thought made him wince. Was he? Dammit, he worked hard. He made a difference. Not everyone could be a hero.

Like Elsa.

There was a knock on the door and Maggie bustled in, her arms full of gear for him, her face set in prim disapproval.

'Dr McCrae's sent you the telephone and the laptop. You can use our phone tonight but she's organising Jason to see you tomorrow. There's also medication, but she says you don't want it. I dare say you'll try and sleep and then be asking me for it in a couple of hours when I'm busy with something else.'

'Are you busy?' he asked, but a sharp look was all he got for his pains.

'It's looking to be a big night.' She sniffed.

'Problems?'

'Nothing that need concern you.'

'I'm a doctor,' he said gently, probing to get past antagonism. 'If absolutely necessary I could get up and help.'

That produced a snort.

'I mean it.'

'You might well,' she snapped as she set her gear down on his tray. 'But a lot of help you'd be. One of our pregnant mums has just come in threatening to deliver, and she's only thirty-two weeks. The smoke on the mainland means she can't be evacuated, so Elsa has her hands full trying to keep that baby aboard. What use is a cardiologist with a broken leg?'

'No help at all,' he said humbly. 'Maggie...'

'Yes.' She tugged up the blood pressure machine and started taking his obs.

'Could you please give me the painkillers Elsa's written up?'

'She says you don't want them until later.'

'I didn't think I did,' he admitted. 'But it's true I'm hurting now, and if I take them then I'll go to sleep and won't need to disturb you later.'

She fixed him with a look of distrust. 'Why the change of heart?'

'Because I'm starting to realise that I need to lie here and be no trouble to you at all.'

'If you need us, we'll come,' she said shortly. 'Ignoring pain, ignoring any other worrying symptom might lead to more drama.'

'Then I won't ignore pain or any other worrying symptom,' he promised. 'But if it's humanly possible, for all our sakes I will cause no more drama.'

CHAPTER SEVEN

ON FRIDAY HE SLEPT. Which infuriated him. Every time he woke he found another two or three hours had drifted by. He'd stir when the nurses came to do his obs, or when his meals turned up. He was extraordinarily hungry, but meals simply seemed to make him sleepier. Jason arrived and set up his new phone and he managed to stay awake for that. Once he was back online he checked his hospital messages, but none of them seemed worth the effort of replying. He thought about opening his files on the borrowed laptop and doing some work, but that was as far as he got. Someone dropped in pyjamas. Getting rid of his hospital gown seemed important. He donned the boxer shorts but the T-shirt was too much trouble.

He slept.

Mid-afternoon he woke and found Elsa at the end of his bed, checking his chart. She smiled as she saw him stir.

'Excellent,' she told him. 'Your body's had a tough time. It needs sleep to recover and it's taking it. Told you so.'

'You don't need to sound so smug about it.'

'I'm enjoying the sensation of telling a specialist what's what,' she said, grinning. 'Allow me my small satisfaction, Dr Pierce. But all's good here. You can go back to sleep.' And she was gone.

Confused, disconcerted, still half asleep, there seemed little choice but to obey, but adding to his confusion was the way Elsa's smile stayed with him while he slept.

Some time in the long distant past, when he was little more than a toddler, he'd had a nanny he'd loved. He had fuzzy memories of being ill and his nanny bustling in and out of the room, sitting on his bed, reading to him, cuddling him.

For some strange reason, Elsa was providing the same comfort. For over twenty-four hours he'd been truly terrified, and the echoes of that terror were still with him. So he slept, but the vision of Elsa stayed with him—Elsa somewhere in the hospital, Elsa checking his obs, Elsa just… here.

It made him feel needy, and he was not needy.

But maybe he was.

He remembered the day that same nanny had left, how useless his tears had been. He'd long got over the idea of needing anyone, but at the moment he seemed to have no choice. He seemed to need to take comfort from her presence. He'd go back to being solitary—of course he would;

nothing else made sense—but Elsa's smile stayed with him as he slept.

It helped.

Friday might have passed in a sleepy haze for Marc, but for Elsa it was far different. Her pregnant patient seemed to have settled for now, but she was still uneasy about her. She checked and checked, and worried and worried. She wanted her evacuated, but smoke haze was still a problem. Meanwhile she had so much work it seemed to be coming out of her ears.

Late at night she did a final round and found Marc awake, but she was too rushed to stay for more than a few moments.

'You're looking good,' she told him. 'Great. Sorry, Marc, but I need to go.'

'It's nine at night. Aren't you done yet?'

'I have a mum bringing in a kid with an ear infection. Why she waited until nine at night to call me… Okay, I know, she was hoping it'd clear by itself because she's so busy. I get it.'

'I wish I could help.'

'Just don't throw out a fever. Go back to sleep.'

'What about your Christmas gifts,' he demanded as she backed out of the door. 'Wrapping? Have you done them yet?'

No. She hadn't. She had to find time. Somehow.

'Bring them to me,' he ordered.

'Really?' She was astonished he'd even remembered.

'Please,' he told her. 'I've slept all day. By tomorrow I'll be bored to snores.'

'You're recuperating.'

'So I need therapy. Bring me what I need.'

She stared at him for a long moment. He was propped up in bed, rumpled with sleep. His arm was in a sling but he'd abandoned the hospital nightwear—he was now wearing decent boxers, but his chest was bare. He was wearing a five o'clock shadow. His dark eyes were smiling and he looked…

Like she had to back out of here now.

'Gifts,' he said, his voice becoming gentle, and she wondered if he knew what highly inappropriate thoughts had just slammed into her head.

'G…gifts,' she managed to echo. 'I'll bring them in the morning.'

She fled.

Saturday morning—Christmas Eve—she was up at five. By nine she felt as if she'd done a whole day's work, but there was more than a day's work still ahead of her.

Mid-morning she checked on Marc, to find him propped up in bed waiting for her and demanding his 'therapy'.

'Okay, you asked for it,' she managed and half

an hour later his room was crowded with gifts, scissors, paper, cards, list and tape. She put the Do Not Disturb sign outside his door and left him staring in some bemusement at what he'd let himself in for.

At midday she snagged his lunch from the kitchen, plus sandwiches for herself, and went to see how he was getting on.

She found him surrounded by a sea of wrapping paper, with a pile of oddly wrapped gifts beside the bed.

He had a geranium on the bed beside him and he was glowering at it.

'Wow,' she said, surveying the chaos from the door. 'This is fantastic. How many have you done?'

'Twenty-six,' he said darkly. 'And *done* is a very loose word. Wrapping doesn't seem to be my forte.'

She grinned. 'So I'm guessing you always get your nurses to do your dressings?'

'Always.'

'No matter.' She perched on the foot of his bed and picked up his chart. 'I'm an appalling wrapper too, so the islanders won't notice any difference.' She took a moment while she read the chart, and then she beamed. 'Good boy, no surprises here.'

'Tell me about your pregnant patient?' he asked, and she screwed up her nose.

'The smoke's cleared so finally we can evacuate her,' she told him. 'Things look like they're settling but I still don't like it and I don't want a thirty-two-weeker delivered here. I've had it happen before when the family wouldn't accept advice.' She hesitated and he saw trauma, tightly held. Then she gave one of her characteristic nods and moved on. 'Well, my advice is stronger now, or maybe it's not even advice. Erica's out of here. The plane's due at three. That's what I needed to tell you. They'll take you too, if you want to go.'

And that took him aback. He could leave. He'd be back in Sydney tonight.

To what?

His mates were in St Moritz, or scattered for the Christmas holidays—either that or they'd be on duty, working their butts off. If he was evacuated he could be admitted into the hospital where he worked. There he'd suffer teasing by the staff, plus—heaven forbid—jovial visits by the elderly consultant who always played Santa. Or he could sit at home with his leg immobile and feel sorry for himself.

Oh, for heaven's sake, what was he thinking? He was involved in an immense international research project. There was always work to do.

But he still might feel sorry for himself, he

conceded, and he glanced up and saw Elsa watching him with what looked like understanding.

'Conflicted, eh?' she asked. 'If you go home you'll realise how much you're missing St Moritz, and you still need bed rest. You know you're welcome to stay here. We can keep you as an inpatient for a couple more days and then you can take the regular flight home. Oh, and you needn't worry about being bored. If you finish these I have a hundred paper napkins I need folding into the shape of little bells. Origami at its finest.'

'Bells...' he said faintly.

'It's only fair to warn you,' she told him cheerfully, 'before you make a decision. So your choice is a nice quiet flight back to Sydney, with well-trained medics to keep you safe, or a hundred paper bells followed by total chaos on Christmas Day. Maybe I didn't mention that as a hospital patient you get to be first on the guest list at our Christmas dinner. We can organise you a wheelchair if you'd like to go.'

'A wheelchair?' he said, revolted.

'A wheelchair it is until that swelling goes down and we can replace that back slab,' she said, in a voice that brooked no argument. 'So, Dr Pierce, what shall it be? You want to share our island Christmas, or do you want to make a run for it? Make up your mind because the evac team needs to know.'

She was smiling down at him, her head cocked slightly to one side like an impertinent sparrow. He found himself smiling back.

Christmas here—or Christmas in Sydney.

Christmas alone—or Christmas with Elsa.

It wouldn't be Christmas with Elsa, he told himself. He was simply one of her many patients.

Still…

'I will help you with the napkin bells if you decide to stay,' she told him generously and he thought of her sitting beside him, that glorious head of fiery curls bent over origami bells. He thought of her smile.

The decision seemed to be made for him.

Christmas with Elsa it would be.

What was he thinking? He was shocked at the direction his errant thoughts were taking. Was this some type of Stockholm Syndrome, where the captive fell for the captor?

Um, that might possibly be overplaying a broken leg and a hospital bed, he conceded, and actually Elsa had freed him, not captured him.

So was it gratitude he was feeling?

Of course it was gratitude, he told himself with a certain amount of relief. It had nothing to do with the way Elsa was smiling at him now, with that inquisitive, intelligent sparrow look. The look that said whatever he decided would be okay by her.

The look that said that, regardless, if he got on that plane she'd fold all hundred napkins herself, and then see patients and take care of her grandpa and get up on Christmas morning and do a ward round and lug these crazily wrapped gifts across to the footy hall and have fun.

Fun. There was the hub of the matter. He looked down at his pile of weird gifts and thought he wanted to be there when they were all opened.

'So what's your decision?' she asked gently, as if she guessed he was torn.

'I'll stay.'

'Wow, that's good of you.'

He grinned ruefully. 'Sorry. If it's okay with you, if you don't need my bed for someone else, if it's okay for me to join in your Christmas festivities...'

'Then you're very welcome. Now, about this geranium...'

'It's too...'

'Too big.' She smiled, a lovely, uncomplicated smile that said all was right with her world. 'The lady gave me a three-inch cutting and I had to carry it home in wet tissue and hope. And here it is, knee high and covered with flowers. When it started growing I had visions of it taking over the whole island—I had to check with our quarantine officer that it was okay to keep it. If we join two sheets together...you plonk it on the wrapping paper and hold it steady and I'll gather the paper together with a big ribbon at the top. What colour do you reckon? Red? Gold? How about rainbow?'

'Rainbow,' he said, slightly shocked as she hauled gaudy bows out of a box and laid them on his bed for his consideration. Memories stirred of elegant gifts in the past, mostly wrapped by the expensive stores they were purchased from. He didn't think he'd ever had a gift that looked so…so…

'How about that for Christmassy?' Elsa demanded as she finished attaching her bow and stood back to inspect their handwork. Scarlet Santa paper and a vast rainbow bow. The whole thing looked more like a scrunched ball of waste paper than elegant gift wrapping. 'Haven't we done well?'

'Very well,' he agreed faintly, and she grinned and touched his shoulder—a fleeting touch— doctor reassuring patient?

'You're doing good, Dr Pierce,' she told him. 'Grandpa will help me sneak these out later. Meanwhile you need to take a nap and gather strength for the bells.'

'Did you say a hundred?'

'Yep,' she said cheerfully, and then added, 'Nope, make that a hundred and one because we just added you to the guest list.'

CHAPTER EIGHT

Christmas Day

SHE REMEMBERED CHRISTMAS as a kid. There had been those first appalling ones with her dysfunctional mother—thankfully mostly a blur now. She did remember the last of those, waking to find her mother surfacing after yet another binge, with nothing planned, nothing to eat, nothing at all.

Her mother had simply forgotten it was Christmas—or hadn't thought of it in the first place.

And then somehow her mother had disappeared, and when her grandfather had swooped in to claim her Christmas had suddenly been magical. Yes, Grandpa had often been called out, but if she wasn't called on to 'help' in the hospital kitchen—she'd been chief taster—or if she didn't need to ride her brand-new scooter or play with her brand-new science kit, she'd go with him. And it seemed every single islander would be celebrating, welcoming her with hugs and mince pies and more sweets than one small kid could possibly consume.

Her island. Her people.

She did love this place, she conceded. Yes, sometimes she resented its demands, but she still remembered that first Christmas on the island, the feeling of being loved unconditionally, of being protected. Of belonging.

And today…

For a few indulgent moments after she woke she let herself stay where she was and just wallowed in the surge of excitement that was Christmas. The restlessness that had been with her for months seemed to have receded. Life was okay. It was Christmas and she was with the people she loved.

And Marc was here.

'But that has nothing to do with it,' she told herself out loud—or if it did it had no business doing so. This was Christmas excitement only. Marc would be gone tomorrow or the day after and she'd be left with…

Tony?

No, not Tony. She'd cleared that up—she hoped. One unwise date…

And that was the problem. The whole island seemed to be watching her, waiting for her to date. Plus all the rest. The islanders would like her to be even more wedded to the island than she was now. When eligible tourists rocked in—the male, single variety—she could almost see their collective nervousness. No one was to take away their Dr McCrae.

Which was fine with her, she conceded, because she had no intention of leaving. She owed the island too much. She loved the island too much.

However…

However, the pool of available islanders as life partners was limited, to say the least. Most of the young ones departed as soon as they could. There were maybe ten unmarried guys around her age on the whole island, and compared to most of them Tony looked good.

Wow, where were her thoughts going? There was a despondent thought to wake up to on Christmas morning. Did she need a reason to get up?

Of course she didn't. She struggled to retain the surge of excitement she'd woken with. She had a good life. A great life. She was the island doc. She didn't need to be anything more.

Except here was this gorgeous guy called Marcus, who'd fallen down a hole, who'd helped her wrap gifts and who'd smiled at her.

Get a grip, she told herself. She was indulging in a teenage fantasy, and she had no time for fantasies today. Grandpa would be heating panforte in the fire stove oven, waiting with a gift for her. Sherlock would be demanding a fast walk before she started work for the day. She needed to do a ward round. She needed to make sure of the final touches to the Christmas dinner.

And her fantasy?

'Marc's as real as Santa Claus,' she said out loud. 'Okay, he's flesh and blood and he'll be staying longer than a quick flit down the chimney, but not much longer. Put your sensible boots on, Dr McCrae, and get to work.'

Marc was accustomed to the extravagant Christmas décor of St Moritz at its glitziest, but the simple Gannet Island hall was a sight to take a man's breath away.

A giant gumtree stood behind the building, laced right to its tip with the island's delicate mistletoe. Who needed bought decorations with such crimson beauty at hand? Massive swathes of the brilliant clusters had been brought inside, creating an effect much more gorgeous than any commercial effort. The hall looked lovely and over a hundred people were set to enjoy themselves.

It seemed that what had begun years before as a Christmas party for hospital patients and for islanders who had no one to share with had grown. Elsa had told him that most island families organised their own Christmas dinner, but still almost all put their names in the ballot to attend this one. The ballot was for entire families, and if the family succeeded in the ballot then this party seemed to be the preferred option.

It meant the party wasn't just for the ill and the lonely. It was a true celebration.

The footy ground was right by the hospital. A couple of beefy footballers were in charge of patient transport, for anyone well enough to enjoy the day. Despite Marc's protests, they'd brought him in a wheelchair—'If you think I'm letting you use crutches before your shoulder's settled you can think again,' Elsa had told him sternly, so now he was seated at one of six vast trestle tables surrounded by…fun.

As everyone walked in they were presented with a hat. These weren't your typical novelty Christmas hats bought in bulk from a cheap supplier. These were knitted or crocheted beanies. Crazy beanies.

'They're an island project,' the guy sitting beside Marc told him. 'We no sooner finish one year's lot than we start another. It's called the Crazy Cap Club. We meet at the school hall every Thursday night and egg each other on to see who can crochet the craziest one.'

'You do it too?' Marc asked, fascinated. The guy he was talking to was an ex-fisherman who'd introduced himself as Wally, in a wheelchair that matched Marc's, in his eighties, a hospital patient with oxygen-dependent emphysema. Weathered from a life at sea, gruff, matter-of-fact, the thought of him with a crochet hook had Marc hornswoggled.

'Doc bullied me into it,' he told Marc. 'I was that tired of sitting on me bum all day, so she gave me a challenge. Do one with a fish on it,' she told me. 'So I did. First one was a bit wobbly but Martin Crosby got it and still wears it out on his boat. That was three years back. This year my one's over on Hazel Mitchell's head. See…the octopus with the tentacles made into braids that hang down her back looking like hair.'

Marc looked and looked again. He'd met Hazel—she was the prim hospital administrator who'd helped him fill in admission forms. She was wearing a very proper skirt and matching jacket—in prim pink. Sensible court shoes and stockings.

And an octopus hat with braids.

And then Elsa came swooping over to their table. He'd been watching her—of course he had. She seemed to be everywhere, hauling people into conversations, rearranging seating. He'd seen her take one old lady who was shrinking at the end of a noisy table and almost literally sweep her up and deposit her in the midst of another table, which seemed just as noisy but the people there seemed to know her. They shoved along to accommodate her and were currently in the midst of swapping hats to figure which hat best suited who. She was giggling and sipping champagne and Elsa had moved on.

'I think your hat's the best,' she told Wally now, stooping to give him a hug, careful, Marc noted, not to bump the oxygen tube that obviously kept the old man alive. 'An octopus with dreadlocks… where will you go from there?'

'I'm thinking of a fisherman with fishhooks and fish dangling,' Wally told her, grinning. 'I got the pattern just about worked out. It'll take me all year to make but it's worth it. You know Muriel Cuthbert got last year's mermaid and she's using it as a tea cosy. Pride of place on the kitchen table, she tells me, and everyone admires it.'

'And why wouldn't they?' Elsa demanded, looking at the hats on both their heads. Wally was wearing a Santa with seven elves stitched into the side. Marc was wearing a particularly mean-looking barracuda. 'Very fetching,' she said, grinning.

Elsa was wearing a pink confection, a crocheted merry-go-round, complete with little horses. It looked complex, weird, adorable.

Marc looked at Elsa's flushed, laughing face and thought he'd never seen anything more beautiful.

It must be the champagne, he thought. He imagined his friends, many of whom would be sipping their hugely expensive Christmas egg-nogs in front of a roaring fire at the resort in St Moritz. They'd all be wearing après-ski wear, very chic.

Elsa was wearing a flouncy red skirt that looked as if it could well be homemade and a crisp, sleeveless blouse. She'd accessorised with a necklace of red tinsel and Santa Claus earrings. Plus her crazy hat. She'd braided her flaming curls and the two braids hung over her shoulders, tied at the ends with red and gold Christmas ribbon.

This was more Christmas cliché than he'd dreamed possible on one woman. Who knew it could look so great?

She was chuckling as she reached over and grabbed Wally's bon-bon. 'I can't believe you haven't pulled it yet!' Inside was a corny joke. She read it aloud to the table, and there was a roar of laughter.

'You guys take care of Marc,' she told every-one. 'He's had a very hard time so it's your re-sponsibility to make him feel better.' And then she grinned. 'And don't be mean,' she added. 'Not one person is to mention hikers and satel-lite trackers and letting people know where you're going. Not one of you. It's Christmas. Cut the guy some slack.'

There was more laughter, all of it friendly, and

Marc was seamlessly pulled into the general conversation.

Elsa hugged Wally and she moved on.

Marc wouldn't have minded a hug himself, he thought.

He was her patient. The way he was feeling was totally inappropriate.

Maybe it *is* Stockholm Syndrome, he thought.

But he didn't feel like a victim.

It was time to turn his attention to eating, and the food was magnificent. The turkeys had arrived—somehow they'd been organised to be delivered on the evacuation flight. That must have been down to Elsa, he thought. How many medics had to juggle the needs of patients with the need for turkeys?

He watched Elsa and thought that this wasn't about her patients or, if it was, her patients were the whole island.

Between main course and pudding there was entertainment. Christmas carols were sung in three-part harmony, led by the local choir, with everyone joining in. A weathered fisherman with a hat and a rabbit made corny magician jokes. A group of elderly ladies in twenties gear danced the Charleston with gusto. At the end of the dance each of the ladies grabbed an unsuspecting diner and dragged them up to join them. Elsa was one of the first to be grabbed, and she Charlestoned with the best of them. Of course she would, he thought, dazed. She was magnificent.

And then there were the gifts. He watched Sandra Carter gasp and flush with pleasure as she removed his dodgy wrapping from around her geranium. He watched the hall roar with laughter as little May Trent opened her 'Beware, Vicious Dog' sign. May giggled and showed the sign to the little dog under her chair, and he thought her Christmas had been made. It seemed the same for every gift recipient.

Thanks to Elsa.

She had him enthralled. When the meal was done and his footballer escorts decreed it was his turn to be wheeled back to the hospital, he looked for Elsa and saw she was already helping clear, chuckling with the locals as she worked. She looked busy and happy. And he thought that he really wanted to stay. Here. Now.

To do what? Help with the dishes? Ha.

He was a patient, an outsider, a visitor who'd already caused everyone massive inconvenience. He submitted meekly to being wheeled back to his ward, to his bed.

He'd missed a call from Kayla. It was early morning in St Moritz. He imagined how Christmas would play out over there—the magnificent, sophisticated Christmas he'd thought was perfect—and decided he hadn't missed it one bit.

'How's the leg?' Kayla's enquiry was perfunctory when he returned the call, and he wondered if she really cared. Was this just a duty phone call?

'It's set and healing. I should be back in Sydney in the next couple of days.'

'That's good,' she told him and then proceeded to outline all her very exciting plans for the holiday.

'Kayla...' he said as she finished.

'Yes?' And he heard the reservation. Did she think he was going to ask her to do something different, mess with her plans?

'Kayla, this isn't working,' he said gently. 'I just thought...while you're over there having fun... please don't think you need to be loyal to me. I think we both know that shouldn't happen.'

There was a silence. He could almost see her sharp mind processing, considering ramifications.

'I guess that's logical,' she said at last. 'You and I...we have had fun.'

'We have.'

'But it was never serious.'

'It never was.' It never had been, he thought. He didn't do relationships, or not the type of relationship he'd seen some of his colleagues fall into. The type where there was co-dependence.

And Kayla was the same. He heard a sigh and

he thought he detected relief. The sound of moving on.

'I'll admit I might have more fun here if everyone stops treating me as poor Kayla who's pining for her boyfriend,' she admitted.

'I can't imagine you pining over anyone.'

'It's not my style,' she agreed, and chuckled.

She really was a friend. Just a colleague.

No longer an occasional lover.

'Okay, then, I'm off to enjoy Christmas,' she told him. 'I hope someone gives you pudding, though I can't imagine it'll come anywhere near what they'll give us here. Poor you. But take care of yourself, Marcus. Bye-ee.'

And she was gone.

What was gone with her?

The knowledge that he wanted to be part of that set? He might well want to, he thought, as soon as he got back to Sydney. As soon as he brushed off the dust of this island.

As soon as he stopped thinking of one gorgeous doctor, dancing through Christmas.

And, as if on cue, there was a knock on his door and the doctor in question appeared.

She was still wearing her gorgeous red skirt and her crazy hat. She had a white coat over the top.

'Good evening, Doctor,' he said, and she grinned.

'Thank you,' she told him. 'A bit of professional respect, that's what I like. Every single patient on my list tonight has greeted me with caution, like I might prescribe enemas instead of antibiotics. Even though I swear the only alcohol I had was in the brandy sauce.' It was said with indignation, followed by a chuckle and if he'd been entranced before he was more so now.

Enthralled, even?

She took his chart from the end of the bed and read it while he watched her. Her chuckle had faded but there was still a trace of a smile on her face. Or maybe that dimple was a permanent feature.

This chameleon doctor, who trekked with her beagle, who'd abseiled down a hole to rescue him, who operated with competence, who'd made Christmas happy for so many...

'This is great,' she said as she hung the chart up again. 'And you're the end of the line. Not a single spike in temperature for the whole hospital, not even an unexpected tummy ache. Christmas has been a success.'

'It's been a success for reasons other than lack of medical repercussions,' he told her. 'You've done great.'

'We've done great,' she corrected him. 'The whole island. Even you with your wrapping.'

'*Even* me?' He managed to sound wounded.

'I mean especially you,' she said and grinned. 'Of course.'

Wow, she was gorgeous. Dammit, why was he in this bed?

'Elsa, when this is all over, if we can organise it, can I see you again?' he asked before he knew he was going to say it. Certainly before he'd thought it through.

It was dumb and she reacted accordingly. There was no hesitation in her response. 'There's no way that's likely to happen,' she told him bluntly. Was he imagining it, or did he hear a note of regret in her voice? 'In a couple of days you'll be out of here.'

'I could stay.' He still had two weeks' leave.

That brought a rueful smile. 'What, and hike on that leg? Not a hope. You'd be stuck in the local guesthouse, bored to snores.'

'But I could take you out to dinner.'

'Which would lead where?' She shrugged and he saw her dredge up a smile from somewhere. Trying to keep it light. 'Marc, you and I both know the rules. Doctors don't hit on patients. Patients don't hit on doctors. Especially when both of them are full of Christmas punch.'

'Asking you out to dinner isn't exactly hitting on you.' He felt like swearing. He was at such a disadvantage, sitting in bed in his borrowed pyjamas. Thankfully, they weren't Linus Larsen's purple ones, but persuading this woman to go out with him could well take more finesse than even the finest pyjamas conveyed. Someone had found him a shirt and loose trousers to wear to dinner but he'd put his pyjama boxers and T-shirt back on when he'd returned to bed. Now he wished he hadn't, but he also knew it wouldn't have made a blind bit of difference what he wore.

'Dating is encompassed in the same rules,' she said firmly. 'Thanks, Marc, but no. I don't do casual dating.'

'Does it have to be casual?' Again it was said before he thought it through, and he winced even as the words came out. Was he talking about being serious? *Now?* He saw her withdraw a little and any last vestige of her smile vanished.

'You have a girlfriend.'

'I don't.' He needed to clear this up. 'Things between Kayla and me were pretty much over even before this happened. This accident's just made our split formal.'

'What, she dumped you because you couldn't go to St Moritz?' She sounded incensed.

'No, it was a mutual dumping,' he told her, 'of a tepid relationship. Maybe like the relationship the nurses tell me you have with Tony.'

She stared at him in astonishment. 'You've been gossiping.'

'I was encouraged to talk while my bed was made,' he said virtuously. 'And talking involves questions. The nurse was very pleased with my progress.'

That won a chuckle, but then her voice turned rueful. 'Well, I wish the dumping could be mutual. Tony's a local kelp farmer, dependable, stolid, and after one date he's utterly convinced that we can marry and raise a whole lot of little kelp farmers.' She sighed. 'But, moving on, your love life is nothing to do with me, and vice versa. Maybe if I'm over in Sydney on a case we can catch up, but you staying for two weeks just so we can date… It's not going to happen.'

'Why not?' He knew his approach was clumsy, but he was struggling here.

'Because at the end of the two weeks you'd go back to Sydney and I…' She hesitated and he saw a struggle to be honest. And honesty won. 'I could get even more unsettled than I am now.'

His gaze met hers and held it for a long moment. She tilted her chin and then dropped it.

'So tell me,' he said gently. 'Elsa, why are you unsettled?'

Maybe it was the brandy sauce. Or maybe it was because it was the end of a long day and she was still riding a wave of confidence.

Or maybe it was because it was Christmas and she was relaxed and he was just *there*.

Regardless, he saw her hesitate and then shrug and decide to go for it.

'Because this island has seven hundred residents and it's too darned small,' she told him, and then she closed her eyes and shook her head. 'No. That's not fair. Gannet Island is what it is. It's always been remote, and I knew what I was in for when I came back here.'

'You came back for your grandpa?'

'I came back because this is my home. Because the islanders are my family. Because they've loved and supported me from the moment I arrived here aged all of seven, so how could I possibly leave them now? I can't, and mostly it's okay except when I think maybe I wouldn't mind dating and having fun and being taken out to a restaurant where the proprietor doesn't skip the bill as long as I give him a consult on the way out as to how to manage his hormonal teenage daughter, or what to do with his infected toe.'

'That happens?' he asked, stunned, and she managed a wry smile.

'Of course. If you stayed, and if we did go out to dinner, it's just as likely to end that way. With you patiently waiting while I head out to the kitchen to watch someone take off his boot.'

'Elsa...'

'It's fine,' she said, and there was another of her wry shrugs. 'I'm over it. Though sometimes I wonder if it'd be nice to be...just normal. But that's my problem, Dr Pierce, not yours.'

'But…'

'No buts.' She hesitated and then forged on again, totally honest. 'You know, I do think you're lovely,' she told him. 'That's a totally unprofessional thing to even think, much less say…'

'The feeling's mutual.'

'Thank you.' Another of her brisk nods. 'That does my ego a whole lot of good, and I'll take it as another Christmas gift. But that's all. Your life's in Sydney and my life's here. There's not the faintest possibility, even if dating came to something…something more…that anything could come of it.'

'So you'll cut me off at the pass now?'

'I have no choice.' She met his gaze again, calm and direct. It was supposed to be a look of acceptance but behind that…he knew pain when he saw it. Almost involuntarily, he swung himself out of bed, steadying on his good leg.

'Elsa…'

'Don't you try and stand,' she said, alarmed. 'What if you fall? And I don't need this. Please. Back off, Marc.'

'Can you really say what you don't need? Or want?' He was balancing but only just. He took her hand and held on. One push and he'd be back on the bed.

But Elsa wasn't pushing. She stared down at their linked hands and he saw her lips quiver.

There was an ache there, he thought. An ache that matched his?

'Don't,' she whispered.

'Do you really want me not to?'

'No. I mean…'

'Elsa, professional ethics or not, impossibility or not, I'd really like to kiss you.'

She closed her eyes for a moment and then looked up at him. Her gaze questioning. 'For Christmas?'

'If you need an excuse.'

'Marc, kissing you would be totally illogical.'

'Like any of the weird and wonderful gifts you've organised for everyone else this Christmas,' he told her. 'Where's your Christmas gift, Elsa?'

And that actually brought a smile. Her eyes suddenly danced with laughter. 'You're saying a kiss from you is equal to a black geranium?'

'Better.'

'Wow,' she said, and suddenly those dancing eyes met his and something changed.

'You'd have to prove it.' Her voice was suddenly decisive.

'Watch me try,' he told her and proceeded to do just that.

What she was doing broke every doctor-patient rule in the book.

Only it was Christmas and she didn't care. The

moment his mouth touched hers she felt herself melting. She felt all sorts of things slipping away.

Mostly common sense.

She was standing in a patient's room. Her patient was in boxers and a T-shirt, balanced on one leg. He had a gammy shoulder. He should have his arm in a sling, but he had both hands on her waist. He'd tugged her close, so her breasts were moulding to his chest.

His mouth was on hers. Strong, warm, demanding. Totally, totally inappropriate.

Totally, totally delicious.

No.

It was more than delicious, she thought dazedly. It was wonderful. Magical.

She'd been kissed before—of course she had. Tony wasn't the only guy she'd dated.

It had never felt like this.

The way he held her…the strength of his hands on her waist…the way he'd hesitated as his mouth found hers, as if checking that this was indeed what she wanted…

How could he doubt it? Her lips opened under his and she felt as if she'd been catapulted into another world.

A world where heat met heat. Where desire met desire.

Oh, she wanted him. She ached for him. Her whole body felt as if it was surrendering.

She was surrendering.

She was being kissed and she was kissing. He didn't need to balance on his bad leg because she was holding him.

Maybe it could count as therapy, she thought, almost hysterically. Helping patient stand. Maybe this *was* a medical tool designed to make him feel better.

It was surely making *her* feel better. Every sense seemed to have come alive. Every nerve-ending was tingling.

More. Every single part of her was screaming that she wanted this man, she needed this man, that she wouldn't mind in the least if they fell back on the bed and…

Um, not in a million years. Not!

Because she didn't want it?

Because this was a hospital ward and any minute the door could open as a nurse arrived for routine obs. This was a patient and she was a doctor and…

Shut up, Elsa, she told her inner self fiercely. Just let this moment be.

So she did. Her mind shut down and she let herself just kiss. And be kissed.

The kiss was deep and long and magical, and as it finally ended—as all kisses surely must— it was as much as she could do not to weep. But Marc was still holding her. He had her at arm's length now, smiling into her eyes with such tenderness that…

No! She made a herculean effort to haul herself together. This was way past unprofessional. She could just about get herself struck off the medical register for this.

Right now she was having trouble thinking that it mattered, whether she was struck off or not. For Marc was smiling at her, and that seemed to be the only thing that mattered in the whole world.

But this was still well out of order. This man's life was in Sydney. It could only ever be a casual fling with a guy who was bored.

Oh, but his smile…

'About that date…' he ventured, and she needed to shake her head but all she could do was look up into his dark eyes and sense went right out of the window.

But then reality suddenly slammed back with a vengeance. The hospital speaker system crackled into life and she heard Kim, one of the hospital's junior nurses. Even through the dodgy hospital intercom she heard the fear in Kim's tone. 'Code Blue. Nurses' station. Code Blue.'

Code Blue!

What was happening with Marc was pure fantasy. This was the reality of her life.

She was out of the door and she was gone.

CHAPTER NINE

WHAT WAS HE supposed to do—go back to bed?

Code Blue was hospital speak almost the world over for 'Get here fast because someone's dying'. Usually it meant cardiac infarct—heart failure.

He was a cardiologist. A heart surgeon.

He was a patient. He was wearing matching boxer and T-shirt pyjamas.

The wheelchair was still beside the bed, left there by the footballer who'd brought him back from lunch. 'No one seems to need this, mate. You might as well keep it; it'll let you get around a bit.' He glanced at it and discarded the idea almost instantly. It was too clumsy. It'd take too long.

He had no crutches but even if he did he'd be no use to anyone if his shoulder slipped out again. There were rails all along the corridor so ambulant patients could practise their walking. 'I'm ambulant,' he said out loud, and managed to hop to the door, grab the rail with his good hand and proceed to demonstrate just how ambulant he really was.

It wasn't hard to find the source of the Code

Blue. Less than a minute's hobbling had him reaching a turn in the corridor to see a cluster of people outside the nurses' station.

He could see two nurses, one with a crash cart, another kneeling. Someone on the floor.

Elsa was also kneeling, her crimson skirt flared around her.

'Grandpa,' she breathed, and his world seemed to still.

He'd met Robert McCrae—of course he had. The elderly doctor had given him the anaesthetic while Elsa had set his leg, and he'd chatted to him a couple of times over the last couple of days. In his late seventies, he'd thought Robert looked a bit too thin, a bit too pale. Marc had had every intention of cornering him before he left and casually offering a full heart check. 'Just to reassure Elsa...' he'd planned to say.

It was too late now. Or was it? 'Grandpa...' Elsa murmured again, and there was a hoarse whisper in response.

'I'll be fine, girl. Don't fuss.'

Not dead. Marc had been present at so many cardiac deaths. Why did this seem so personal? Why was his relief so profound?

'You weren't breathing.' That was the nurse by the crash cart. She looked as if she was about to burst into tears.

'Let me up. Give me a hand, girl,' Robert attempted to snap at Elsa, but the snap was little more than a whisper and Elsa was having none of it. She had the portable defibrillator at hand, and before he could argue she'd ripped his shirt open.

The old guy could scarcely breathe but he was still indignation personified. 'This is my best shirt.'

'Ex shirt,' she told him. 'Kim doesn't make mistakes, and if she said you stopped breathing then you stopped breathing. And you were still unconscious when I got here.'

'I just got a bit dizzy, that's all.'

'I'm fitting the pads in case we need them,' she told him. 'You know you'd do the same for any patient with collapse and a history of cardiac problems.' She looked up. 'Kim, contact Geoff and Ryan. Tell 'em we need to lift a prostrate patient...'

'Prostrate?' It must be hard to sound outraged when there was clear difficulty in breathing, but Robert managed it.

'And you'll stay prostrate until I say otherwise,' Elsa told him, bossiness underpinned with a definite shake in her voice. 'You taught me to be bossy in a crisis, Grandpa, so don't you fight me when I follow your orders.'

'It's not a crisis.' But he'd had enough. He'd been trying to lift his head. Now he slumped back and let his protests die to nothing.

'Elsa, would you let me help?'

She was fitting the pads of the defibrillator. Designed to jerk the heart back into motion when it stopped, it wasn't necessary now that Robert was conscious, but the elderly doctor had clearly lost consciousness, had clearly fallen. There was something else going on here. If there'd been a blockage then it could block again at any minute, and seconds would be precious.

She finished fitting the pads and then turned to Marc. 'Go back to bed,' she said quietly.

'Elsa, I have a broken leg, not the plague. You have a cardiologist on site, and I may well be what your grandfather needs right now. Make use of me.'

He saw her hesitate, torn. Every instinct would be to protect her patient—him. Every desire would be to do what was best for her grandfather.

'Please, then,' she said gruffly, and he could hear the emotion in the two words. Then she turned back to Robert. 'Grandpa, you remember Marc's here—Dr Pierce? You know he's a cardiologist from Sydney? He's offered to ignore his broken leg and give his opinion.'

'What's he charging?' Robert demanded, and there was a hint of humour in his thready voice that further reassured Marc. He might have lost consciousness for a moment, but the blood supply hadn't been cut off for long enough to cause even minor mental impairment.

'Cut rate special,' he said as one of the nurses moved forward to help him hop from the support of the handrail to where Robert lay. 'You fixed my leg, so I'll have a shot at fixing your heart.'

'Might be a damned sight harder to fix,' Robert growled.

'It might,' Marc said quietly. Robert was still on the floor and he dropped to join him. It was hardly the usual medical scene—patient on floor, doctor dressed in pyjamas also on floor, his back slabbed leg stretched out before him.

He wedged himself around so he was side-on to Robert. Elsa was on the other side and a glance told him the strain she was under. Her face was almost as pale as her grandfather's.

And there was reason. Robert's breathing was fast, shallow, laboured. His skin was bluish, cool to the touch. Marc lifted his wrist and kept his face impassive as he noted the racing pulse. For all his fieriness, his attempt at humour, Robert was looking terrified.

'Pain?' Marc asked and watched him close his eyes for a moment and then decide to be honest.

'Bad,' he conceded. 'Chest. Shoulder. Another bloody heart attack. Must be a minor one this time, though. I'll be all right.'

'You'll have to go back to Sydney,' Elsa managed, and Marc could still hear the tremor. Finding her grandfather unconscious must have been horrific. 'We'll get you stabilised and call for evacuation.'

'Leave things for a moment,' Marc said softly. He was looking further, seeing things he didn't like.

The probability was that this was a heart attack, hopefully small, but there was no guarantee it wouldn't be a precursor to a bigger one. Yes, evacuation was called for, to a hospital with a state-of-the-art cardiac facility, with a team of trained medics on board the flight. But the look on Robert's face… And what was beneath…

He was seeing swollen, bulging neck veins and they were acting like flashing lights to Marc's trained eye. The heart was pumping blood out, but there was some impediment to its return.

'Can I have your stethoscope?' he asked Elsa, and she handed it wordlessly across. He listened to the muffled heart sounds, and his unease deepened.

'Blood pressure?' he asked, and the nurse fitted the cuff.

Low.

'What are you thinking?' It was Robert himself who demanded to know. This was doctor to doctor. There'd be no sugar-coating what he was starting to suspect, and it'd be an insult to even try.

'I'm thinking we need to exclude cardiac tamponade,' he said briefly. 'Your veins are swollen. Low blood pressure. Muffled heart sounds. That's Beck's triad—the three symptoms that make me sound clever when I'm just fitting a pattern to what's happening.'

There was an expletive from Robert, and Marc gave him what he hoped was a reassuring grin.

'Exactly. No sweat though, Robert, because even if I'm right I've coped with cardiac tamponade before and I can cope with it now.'

He glanced up at Elsa then, and saw her face had bleached even whiter. She'd know the risks.

Cardiac tamponade was indeed frightening. Caused by trauma, by cancer or sometimes by a heart attack, fluid or blood built up between the heart and the pericardium, the sac surrounding the heart. The pericardium consisted of two layers of tissue, with a small amount of fluid preventing friction between the layers. If this fluid built up, it put pressure on the heart, affecting its ability to pump blood around the body.

Robert might have just suffered a heart attack, or he might have suffered a minor attack weeks ago. The pressure might have built slowly, finally causing collapse. Or the leak could be recent, the pressure building fast.

Regardless, cardiac tamponade meant there was no time for evacuation. The pressure had to be removed now.

The two guys who worked as occasional orderlies, handymen or gardeners appeared and seamlessly went into action, helping Elsa transfer Robert to a stretcher and then lifting him onto a trolley. One of the nurses helped Marc to his feet. He was swearing inwardly. He wanted two good legs. He wanted to be dressed—at least in the soft shirt and loose gym pants he'd worn to lunch. He wanted to feel professional, fully functional—he *needed* to be at the top of his game. This was a situation he was trained for, and he wanted the capacity to move fast.

'Can you organise an echocardiograph and a chest X-ray?' he asked Elsa. Dammit, he felt helpless. 'And can someone help me get dressed?'

'Marc, you can't…' Elsa's voice trailed off. If the ECG and chest X-ray confirmed the diagnosis, there was no choice and she—and her grandfather—would know it.

'Robert,' Marc said, taking a moment to rest a hand on the shoulder of the elderly doctor, 'you know what's at stake here. If it is indeed tamponade then we need to get the pressure off fast. You'll need to go to the mainland to get any underlying problems with your heart sorted, but the tamponade has to be fixed now. I might be a cardiologist with a gammy leg and a sore shoulder, but that doesn't interfere with my skills. If the echocardiograph confirms my diagnosis you'll need percutaneous drainage and that's a skill I have. Will you let me and your granddaughter make you safe?'

And the old man's hand came up and gripped his, hard. Marc could feel the tremor. He could feel the fear.

'Do what you have to do, son,' Robert managed. 'You seem a damned idiot at bushwalking, but I assume you're not the same in an operating theatre.'

'I'm very good,' Marc told him. This was no time for false modesty. 'I'm who you need right now, gammy leg or not. Trust me.'

'I trust you,' Robert said and the grip on his hand tightened.

'Marc…' It was Elsa, and there was fear in her voice, too.

'And so must you, girl,' Robert said, forcefully now, as he directed his attention to his granddaughter. 'We're lucky to have a cardiologist to hand, even if you did have to crawl underground and sleep with him for a full night to get him here.'

The echocardiograph reinforced Marc's diagnosis. The chest X-ray and ultrasound confirmed it.

Elsa stared at the image on the ultrasound screen and felt ill.

If she'd been on her own here she couldn't have coped. She'd have had to evacuate her grandfather, and with the pressure building in the hours it would have taken to get him to Sydney... The outcome didn't bear thinking of.

And doing such a procedure herself? She knew the principles, but to perform the drainage, especially on someone who was probably compromised with heart damage anyway... When that someone was her grandfather... To insert a needle into such a risky place, to do no damage...

She didn't need to. She had a cardiologist right here. The knowledge made her feel dizzy.

Marc was scrubbing. The nurses had found a stool with wheels and height adjustment. At full stretch it made him tall enough to use the sinks, to operate, to be fully functional.

He looked across at her as Maggie helped him on with theatre gear, and he must have seen the tension.

'It's okay,' he told her gently. 'We have this in hand. We'll try percutaneous drainage first. If that doesn't work then we'll move to the subxiphoid approach—taking away a slice of the pericardium. But I don't anticipate that. We'll give him the lightest possible general—I don't want any more risk to his breathing than he already

has. While you monitor that, then I'll use the ultrasound to guide a nice fat needle into the cav-
ity, set up a catheter and let it drain.'

Said like that it sounded simple. She knew it
wasn't.

'Then we'll move him to Sydney and let the
big boys deal with whatever the underlying cause
is,' Marc told her, his voice calm, reassuring but
firm. She wasn't the doctor here. She wasn't
being asked to make decisions—she was being
told the best course of action for her grandpa.
'Given his history, I'm almost sure this'll have
been caused by another heart attack. Maybe a
small one. There's no sign of neurological impairment. This seems straightforward. For me this is
common or garden repair work, Dr McCrae, so
you can take that fearful look off your face, accept that your grandpa's going to live and turn
into the professional I know you are.'

His gaze was still on her face, his look steady,
strong, sure. *You can do this*, his gaze said. And
I need a doctor, not a whimpering relative.

Right. She could do this.

She must.

And half an hour later the thing was done. A light
anaesthetic. An awful, breath-holding time while
she watched as Marc used the ultrasound wand
to guide the needle into position.

His approach was sure, unhesitating, skilled.

Using an eight-centimetre, eighteen-gauge angiocatheter—thank heaven for the comprehensive surgical kit the island possessed—watching the ultrasound every fraction of an inch of the way, he slowly, skilfully found what he was looking for. When the pericardial sac was entered there was a grunt of satisfaction as the ultrasound showed the needle where he needed it to be. Slowly he advanced the sheath and withdrew the needle. A guide wire was then advanced through the angiocatheter, followed by a dilator and a pigtail catheter.

'Yes!' he said with relief as the fluid started to flow, as the tamponade started to shrink, and that was the first time Elsa heard pressure in his voice. Even though he'd sounded sure, this was a procedure that took skill. Even now. Elsa was monitoring breathing, watching the heart monitor like a hawk, waiting for a reaction. Robert's heart was damaged. Any minute now...

'Not going to happen,' Marc said softly, glancing at the monitor and then her face. 'Fluid's coming off, and things are looking good.'

And so it was. Once the catheter was in place the pericardial fluid drained like a dream. The fluid would be submitted for culture and cytological analysis, checking for signs of something other than heart attack—trauma or cancer—but there seemed no sign of either.

She watched on, staring at the monitor as if she could will the heartbeat to strengthen. And it did.

'I'm only draining a thousand mil,' Marc told her. 'I don't want hypotensive shock. But I'm pretty sure it's enough to keep him safe.'

It maybe it was. Robert's heart had returned to a reassuringly normal rhythm. He was breathing on his own now, and when Elsa removed the oxygen his chest rose and fell normally. His colour was returning. He was safe.

For now. There was still the underlying cause to treat.

'I told one of the nurses to arrange evacuation,' Marc said briefly, once again watching her face. 'He'll need more aspirations, usually every four to six hours. We'll do another just as he leaves, and then the cardiac unit in Sydney can take over.' Robert was already stirring. The anaesthetic had been the lightest possible. 'Hey, Robert,' Marc said gently, and he took the old man's hand. 'All done. How do you feel?'

There was silence for a couple of moments while Robert got his bearings, while his world settled. They watched him take conscious breaths, watched him feel his chest expand, watched him realise the pressure was no longer there.

'Beautiful,' he murmured, and Elsa smiled and

smiled and gripped Robert's hands and then decided she needed to wipe away a stupid tear that was tracking down her cheek. Only she couldn't because she was holding onto her grandpa.

And then Marc was leaning over the table and wiping it away for her, smiling at them both. 'Well done, Dr McCrae,' he told her.

'There was nothing well done about it,' she said gruffly. 'Marc operated, Grandpa, not me.'

'And your granddaughter held it together, acted professionally with a brilliant anaesthetic and didn't once behave like you'd scared her out of her wits,' Marc said, still smiling at her. 'But now she needs to act like a relative. Elsa, I want you to go pack for your grandpa and for yourself. Robert, we're evacuating you to Sydney. You know the underlying cause of the tamponade is most likely to have been another heart attack, or complications from the last one. There'll be an emergency physician on board the plane to keep you safe in transit. You'll be assessed fully in Sydney, so you need to be prepared to stay for a while. Hope for the best—maybe another stent— but prepare for a full bypass. That could mean a two-week stay before they let you fly home. Elsa, you know there's relative accommodation at the hospital. When we asked for the evac plane we asked for that to be organised as well.'

'But…' Elsa was staring at him in dismay '… I can't go. Two weeks…'

'You have no choice.'

'When Grandpa had his last attack and had the stent inserted, I was away for two days,' she told him, almost stammering. 'There was no one here to take over. We got away without a disaster that time, but for the island to have no doctor…'

'Elsa'll stay here,' Robert growled. 'There's no need to come with me. It's a fuss over nothing.'

But there was every need. Elsa stared down at her grandpa and saw it in his eyes.

This latest episode would have terrified him. Not being able to breathe… Feeling the pressure build… Oh, thank God for Marc, but the old man wasn't out of the woods yet, and she could see by his face that he knew it.

Yes, there'd be an emergency physician on the plane, but Grandpa needed family beside him. He needed her. She *had* to be with him, but she could see the warring needs on her grandfather's face. He would know the risks. And for there to be no doctor on the island at all…

'You have to stay,' Robert muttered grimly. 'Don't be a fool, girl. You think we can get a locum at this short notice, at this time of year? You know after Christmas half of Australia goes to sleep and the other half goes to the beach until mid-January. Or they come here and break their necks doing damned silly things. You have no choice. I'll be fine, girl.'

But still she saw the fear—and she glanced up at Marc and realised that he'd seen it too.

'There's no need for a locum,' he said gently. 'Aren't you lucky that you already have a resident doctor?'

They both stared at him, their expressions suggesting he'd suddenly grown two heads. 'You?' Elsa stammered, as if such a thing was tantamount to suggesting a five-year-old took over the medical needs of the island.

'Don't look at me as if I'm an idiot,' he told them. 'I know I'm a cardiologist, but I have basic skills as well. I'm sure I can remember the treatment for nice normal things like the common cold. Isn't it to give the patient honey and lemon drinks and it'll cure itself? I can probably cope with that.' He grinned, his smile encouraging them to override their fear.

'Seriously,' he continued, 'you have a great nursing staff. My shoulder's sore but it's firmly back in place and I won't be needing to lift any weights. I know a slightly battered doctor is less than ideal, but it seems a darned sight better than no doctor at all. I have a bung leg but I'll not be running any races. We can organise someone to drive me if I need to go off site. I have the next two weeks off. I know I should be in St Moritz but as far as prestige points go when I finally head back to work, two weeks on Gannet Island with a climbing injury cuts it almost as well.'

'A climbing injury? More like a falling down a hole injury,' Elsa said before she could help herself, and his grin widened.

'Are you intending to mess with my hero image, Dr McCrae?'

'Let him be heroic if that's what's needed for him to stay here,' Robert said gruffly, and reached out and took Marc's hand. 'I'll even sign something to say you fell down the hole saving... what, a kitten? Would that do?'

'A kitten?' Elsa said, astounded.

'He was saving Sherlock then,' Robert said, and the elderly doctor even managed a chuckle. 'Sherlock won't mind sacrificing his pride for the greater good.'

'I'll even take care of Sherlock while you're away,' Marc offered. 'Or Sherlock might take care of me.'

But Elsa wasn't smiling. 'Grandpa, you know I can't leave. We can't ask this of Marc.'

'Let's get this down to basics,' Marc demanded. 'Robert, do you want your granddaughter to come with you?' He fixed Robert with a look that demanded honesty. And the elderly doctor looked from him to Elsa and back again.

He'd know the odds. An underlying heart attack had probably caused the tamponade, and the damage wasn't yet diagnosed. He was still in peril and he knew it.

'I do,' he whispered, and Elsa's face twisted in fear and uncertainty.

'And Elsa, do you want your grandpa to go alone?'

'Of course not. But...'

'Then you have no choice,' Marc said gently.

'I know. But oh, Grandpa...'

'Now don't you make this into a big deal just because I said I need you,' Robert managed. He managed a smile, fighting to recover his pride. 'Love, you know I hate hospital coffee. I'll... I'll need someone to bring me a decent cup a couple of times a day.'

'So there you are,' Marc told her. 'You have two weeks of being personal barista for your grandfather, while a one-legged doctor takes over all your duties on the island. You might need to organise someone else to walk Sherlock, but for the rest... All sorted.'

'Marc...'

'Enough.' He put his hand out and cupped her chin, forcing her gaze to meet his, suddenly stern.

'As your grandpa says, don't make a fuss,' he said softly. 'Just do what you need to do. I suspect your grandpa's coffee needs won't be too extensive. You might even have time to see a bit of Sydney at the same time. You might even have time to have fun.'

Elsa disappeared to pack and probably to do a bit of panicking on the side.

Marc returned to his nice, quiet hospital bed and did a bit of panicking himself. What had he let himself in for? He'd offered to be the island doctor for up to two weeks. A family doctor.

He hadn't done any family medicine since a placement during internship. He remembered minor illnesses, minor injuries, stress, depression, teen pregnancies, the problems of the elderly with multiple health problems. He remembered being hit by an elderly patient because he couldn't justify signing a form saying the old guy could retain his car licence.

'You need to learn to care,' the family doctor he'd been working beside had told him. 'If you genuinely care for your patients, then everything else will follow. Empathy is everything—emotional connection.'

The experience had confirmed Marc's decision to specialise in heart surgery. He'd been raised to be emotionally distant. The idea of providing an emotional connection to his patients seemed impossible.

Elsa had the ability, he thought, remembering

the faces of those who'd received her extraordinary gifts. She had it in spades. Which was why she was a family doctor and he wasn't.

Except now he was, for two weeks.

No one could expect emotional connection in two weeks, he told himself. He'd offered because it was the least he could do—after all, Elsa had saved his life. This would repay a debt. He could see patients in need and then walk away.

And then the door opened, tentatively. It was Maggie. Despite their initial conflict over the Dorothy the Dinosaur tablet, she'd helped care for him, she'd assisted in Robert's surgery with efficiency and he was aware that she was an excellent nurse.

'Are you ready to start work?' she asked.

'What, now?'

'Bradley Norfolk's just fallen off his Christmas trampoline,' she told him. 'It looks like a greenstick arm fracture. Are you up for it?' She eyed him, lying on his pillows, his bedding pulled up to his chin. 'You look like a new intern,' she said bluntly, and she grinned. 'Scared rigid.'

Maybe it was time to pull himself together. He pushed back his covers, sat up and swung his bad leg off the bed.

'We're setting you up with a permanent wheelchair,' she told him. 'With leg support so your leg's out straight.'

'I can manage without a wheelchair.'

'Elsa's orders. She says she doesn't want any more pressure on that arm, and if you're balancing then you're at risk.'

His first reaction was to reject the wheelchair out of hand—he needed to act like a doctor, not a patient. But his shoulder was still painful. Elsa's suggestion was sensible.

He needed to be sensible.

'For today and maybe for tomorrow,' he told Maggie. 'By then I should be able to manage with sticks.' Even that revolted him.

'Very wise,' Maggie said, and her smile widened. 'You know, the islanders have learned it's much easier to do what Doc Elsa says. She's pretty much always right. If you're standing in for her you have pretty big shoes to fill.'

'Just lucky my foot's already swollen then,' he said grimly. 'Maggie, I'm going to need more clothes.'

'Elsa's already given orders,' she told him. 'We're on it.'

'Then Maggie…'

'Yes?'

'It's time for Elsa to stop giving the orders,' he told her. 'From now on, you're stuck with me.'

The evacuation crew oozed medical competence. The doctor in charge listened to Elsa's stuttered explanation, spoke briefly to Robert—and then did a hand-over with Marc.

Marc was in his wheelchair, but his medical competence matched the medic in charge. They exchanged notes, films, cardiographs. Elsa was on the sidelines, holding Robert's hand.

Robert was the patient. Elsa was family.

'Takes a bit of getting used to,' Robert growled. He was on the transfer trolley, waiting to be lifted into the plane.

'Yeah.'

'He'll do good by us. The island's in good hands.' He was trying to reassure her. For heaven's sake…

'I'm sure he will,' she managed, and as she listened to the clipped professional handover between the two men she knew she was right. 'Except…'

'Except Dotty Morrison might have to forgo her placebo pills for a while,' Robert said with a forced chuckle, and Elsa thought of the pills she'd been prescribing for the old lady affected by Alzheimer's for the last few months and grimaced.

'I haven't even told him about that.'

'Told me what?' Finishing his handover, Marc had wheeled himself across to join them.

'Dotty Morrison,' Elsa told him, thinking of all the other things she hadn't told him. 'She has Alzheimer's and high blood pressure. She's struggling to stay at home and her medication's the biggest hurdle—she takes it too often or not at all, but she hates the thought of not being in charge. So now I give her placebos, telling her to take one every morning, one every night. Her daughter comes around twice a day with her 'extra' pills—the real ones—which she tells her are multivitamins. Dotty takes them to humour her, but she knows the ones I prescribe and she gets from the pharmacist are the important ones. She takes them whenever she thinks it might be morning or night and everyone's happy.'

'And they're what? Sugar pills?'

'Sugar pills?' Elsa asked incredulously. 'No such thing. I give her a nice formal script that says "Disaccharide $C_{12}H_{22}O_{11}$, twice daily".'

'Which is sugar.'

'If you're going to be pedantic, then yes,' she said with asperity, 'but don't you dare tell Dotty. I tell her it's to improve cerebral function—she likes that because she knows she forgets things. She takes her script along to the pharmacy, Doug puts her pills in a bottle with her name on and everyone's happy. Except she tends to go through her bottle about once a week and sometimes more, and she loses her repeat scripts so I expect you'll see her soon. Marc, there's so much I haven't told you.'

'He'll be all right, girl,' Robert said, gripping

Marc's hand as the crew prepared to lift him into the plane. 'If he's got his cardiology ticket he must have the brains to prescribe sugar pills and he can always phone you. Thank you, son,' he said and then he was lifted up and away.

The medic crew boarded the plane, busying themselves, fitting Robert with the equipment, the oxygen, the stabilisers he'd need for the journey. Marc and Elsa were finally left alone.

'I don't... I can't think what to say,' Elsa told him.

'Don't say anything. You're not going out of contact. If someone presents at the surgery demanding medication for their leprosy or whatever, I have your number.'

'I can't thank you...'

'And I can't thank you. So let's not.'

'Marc...'

'Just relax. Robert's in good hands. He'll be fine. You might even have a chance of a holiday yourself.'

'If he doesn't need me, I can come home.'

'He will need you. Hospital's a lonely place with no family.' Before she could stop him he'd pushed himself to his feet. Instinctively she reached forward to steady him, but afterwards she couldn't remember whether he'd gripped her hands before she'd gripped his.

Regardless, she gripped and he held, or vice versa.

He was her patient. No, he wasn't her patient now. He was the doctor who'd saved her grandfather's life.

He was Marc.

The three images were blurring. Boundaries weren't being crossed, they were dissolving.

'Your grandpa will be fine,' he said, strongly now. 'I've phoned my boss—he's head of cardiology at Sydney Central. He's promised to take on Robert's care himself and there's no one better. This guy here...' he motioned into the plane, to the medic in charge '...he's the best as well. The only extra Robert needs is family, and in you he has gold. Take care of yourself, Elsa. Come back with a patched-up grandpa but come back rested yourself. I can't think of anyone who deserves a break more.'

'Marc...'

'Just go,' he said softly, but his grip on her hands tightened. 'But I'll be in touch and thinking of you every step of the way.'

She looked up at him, feeling dazed. Too much was happening, too fast.

He was holding her. For support, she told herself frantically but as her gaze met his she knew it was no such thing. His eyes were dark, fathomless, compelling. There was a faint smile, a question—an answer? She couldn't look away.

The question? It was being asked of her and all she had to do was respond. Which was what she did. Almost of their own volition her feet tilted so she was on tiptoe. So lips could meet.

And kiss.

Warmth, heat, strength.

Or maybe it was the opposite of strength. Maybe it was loss of control, for how could she be in control when she was being kissed like this?

Twice in one day. Twice! But this was different.

Behind them were Geoff and Ryan, the hospital orderlies who'd helped load Robert into the ambulance for transport to the runway and were now waiting to take Marc back to the hospital. There were a couple of airport workers round the plane—locals.

News of this kiss would be all over the island before the plane even took off.

But right now she couldn't care less. How could she care? All that mattered was the feel of Marc holding her. He'd saved her grandpa. He was holding her steady. He was her rock.

Her rock with a broken leg. Her rock who was here for only two weeks. He was her rock who was supposed to be in St Moritz right now with his glamorous ex-girlfriend.

She had no right to kiss him, and he had no

right to kiss her. But still she clung for one last, long sweet moment. It was a moment of madness, a moment that she knew must mean nothing, but she took it, she savoured it, she loved it.

And then there was an apologetic cough from behind Marc's shoulder.

'Sorry miss, but we need to get going,' one of the medics called to Elsa. 'You need to board. Don't worry, sir, we'll take good care of them and bring them home safe.'

Home safe... Two lovely words.

But the medic was looking at her with sympathy. He thought he was tearing her away from... her partner? Her lover?

No such thing. She didn't want sympathy, and she didn't...couldn't...want complications.

'I'm ready to go,' she managed, struggling to sound professional, as if she hadn't just been kissed so thoroughly she felt dizzy. 'Thank you for your help, Dr Pierce. I'll see you soon.'

'I hope so,' he said, and lifted the back of his hand to brush her cheek. It was a gesture of farewell, an acknowledgement of times shared, of forced intimacy that was now over, and there was no reason for it to make her feel even more disoriented than she already was.

But disoriented was too simple a word to describe what she was feeling. She needed to join her grandfather in the plane, but turning and walking away from Marc felt wrong.

CHAPTER TEN

'I'VE RUN OUT of pills.'

'Already?' It was just as well he'd been warned. This was the first clinic on Boxing Day—'for urgent cases only'—but Dotty Morrison had insisted she was tacked onto the end of his list.

'I think I might have doubled up,' the little lady said doubtfully. 'What with Christmas and all. But an extra pill or two won't hurt me, will it, Doctor?'

He checked. Elsa's notes were comprehensive and, worded in case Dotty caught sight of them, carefully benign.

'Dr McCrae wrote you a script with five repeats only last week,' he said cautiously. 'Have you used them all?'

'Oh, no, Doctor. It was much longer than a week ago. The chemist says I should leave the script at the pharmacy, but they keep muddling them. I do like to keep an eye on my own medications. It's my body, isn't that right, Doctor? I have a responsibility to care for what goes into it.'

'You certainly do,' Marc said, suppressing a grin as he replaced her script.

She accepted it with grace and checked it with care. 'Thank you, dear,' she told him. 'But you're not as neat as our Dr Elsa.'

'I'm afraid I'm not. I'm not as fast either.' Dottie had been kept waiting three-quarters of an hour for her appointment.

'Well, that's because you've broken your leg,' Dottie said reasonably.

It wasn't exactly that, he thought as he bade the elderly lady goodbye. It was because family medical practice required skills Marc had pretty much forgotten. He'd just had to cope with a teenager whose acne had flared up. She was hysterical because her family was heading to Sydney to meet friends—'and there's this boy...'

He'd had to excuse himself 'to take an urgent phone call' which involved hobbling out to Reception to check current meds for acne, correct dosages, contraindications.

There'd been many 'urgent phone calls' this morning. But finally he was done. He had house calls scheduled for later this afternoon—either Geoff or Ryan would drive him—but he had time to put his leg up for half an hour and field a call from Elsa.

'How's it going?' he asked.

Her voice sounded tense, distracted and he thought *uh-oh*.

'He's okay.'

Then he heard her pause and take a deep breath. 'No. More than okay. The tamponade's pretty much settled—they've stopped the draining.' That made sense. The pericardium had to retain a little fluid to protect the heart. 'But you were right. He's had another heart attack. When pressed, he admitted he'd had what he thought was an event during the night while I was on the mountain with you. It passed and he didn't want to worry me—he said he'd think about it after Christmas. Anyway, he's in the right hands now. He's scheduled for a quadruple bypass late this afternoon, but he's already worrying about the need to spend time here in cardio rehab. His biggest worry is me being here rather than back on the island.'

'And you? Are you worrying about being there rather than back on the island?'

'Of course,' she said simply. 'I can't help it. Have there been any problems?'

'No.'

'Not a one?'

'My biggest hurdle so far has been finding current treatment for teenage acne,' he admitted. 'I had Jess Lowan here, threatening suicide or worse. It seems she's in love with the son of family friends, and how can she face him with zits on her nose?'

'I hope you took it seriously,' she told him. 'Jess is...high strung to say the least.'

'I took it very seriously. The treatment's changed since I was in med school but, thanks to the internet, Jess has now been hit with a barrage of treatment that should effectively nuke every zit before it has a chance to interfere with the course of young love. I just hope he's worth it.'

'Oh, dear. You know she'll be in love with someone else next week.'

'Someone who prefers his women with zits? Then Houston, we have a problem. I see no chance of reversal.'

She chuckled but it sounded strained. 'Seriously though, Marc...'

'Seriously, I'm doing well.' He let himself sound serious too, still hearing the stress in her voice. 'There's been no pressure. I have two house calls to make this afternoon, then a simple ward round, and as long as everything stays quiet I'll be in bed with a book by eight-thirty.'

'When you should be drinking mulled wine with your mates in St Moritz.'

'I'm not missing it a bit.' And as he said it he realised it was true. The situation here was challenging—and he didn't mind this phone call with Elsa. There'd be more of them, he knew. The thought of working as he was doing, of helping her out for two weeks...it wasn't a penance.

'You know things will hot up from today?' Elsa warned. 'The holiday crowds start streaming in on Boxing Day, and they do really dumb things.'

'Like falling down holes.'

'Like falling down holes,' she agreed. 'Though the guys have hiked back up to where you fell and fenced off that whole area, with huge warning signs saying death and destruction for all who enter here. It's a pity we can't do that for every peril on the island. Like the sun. What's the betting you'll have half a dozen cases of sunstroke by this time tomorrow? Our work practically quadruples in the holiday period.'

He thought about that. Today had been relatively quiet—no dramas, a simple clinic and stable inpatients. Still, by the end of the day he'd have worked reasonably hard.

If it quadrupled…

'How do you cope?'

'I have Grandpa.'

'You won't have your grandpa for a few weeks. He's going to need decent rehab. Seriously.'

'Which is why I'll rest up before I come home. I know I need to stay. If I leave Grandpa here he'll be on the next plane after me. But Marc, I'm worrying about you coping.'

'I'll read up on sunstroke before I go to bed tonight.'

'It won't just be sunstroke. You don't have…

I don't know…a friend who could help? Maybe your Kayla? Is she another doctor?'

'She is,' he told her. 'But she's not my Kayla and there's not a snowball's chance in a bushfire she'll cut her holiday short to come here.'

'Another colleague then?' She was clutching at straws. 'If I stay here for two full weeks you will need help.'

'And you'll need help long-term,' he told her. 'At his age and after two heart attacks, it's time for Robert to think of retiring.'

'You think I don't know that?'

'So you need to think about hiring a full-time partner.'

'Like that's going to happen.'

'Why not?'

'Because it's not viable,' she said shortly. 'An island with a population of seven hundred provides a meagre income. The six islands have far too much medical need for me to handle alone, but they're too far apart to service. In an ideal world, with more doctors and a fast ferry service, we could set up a central medical centre on Gannet. But a ferry service requires money the islanders don't have and, even if there was one, no island doctor could make the kind of money I bet you're making in Sydney. Why would anyone come here by choice?'

She caught herself, and he heard her pause

and regroup. 'Sorry. That was uncalled for. The money thing's minor but I am facing the problem that without Grandpa's help…' Her voice trailed off.

'Without his help maybe you need to leave the island?' he said gently. 'It seems harsh but someone else will take your place.'

'I couldn't think of leaving.'

'You need to think about it. With your grandpa's medical needs he'd be much safer on the mainland. And you… You've already said you feel constricted here.'

'But it's *my* island,' she said, suddenly angry. '*My* home. You don't get that?'

'There are lots of other places in the world.'

'Like St Moritz. No, that was mean. But where could I work? In a city clinic so Grandpa could be within cooee of specialist help? We'd both hate that. Or a country practice where my problems would be the same—and I wouldn't be surrounded by family.'

'You'd have Robert.'

'He's only one small part of my family. My family's the whole island. It's home. You must see, Marc…' She broke off and sighed. 'Enough. My future's not your problem and you have your own problems. Acne to sort. A leg that needs resting.'

'The acne's sorted and my leg's resting as we speak.'

'Then rest some more,' she told him. 'I'll return as soon as possible.'

'As soon as the doctors say it's safe for your grandfather to be here?' He hesitated but it had to be said. 'Elsa, there'll always be underlying medical problems. It seems harsh to say it, but I won't be here to help next time.'

She faltered at that, but then gathered herself again. 'That has to be okay. We've managed to cope without you before. Go rest that leg, Marc. Goodbye.'

She abandoned her phone and walked out onto the balcony. The apartments designed for hospital relatives were spartan but the views were fantastic. At least they were fantastic if she stood at the very far end and leaned out. She could even see the Opera House and the harbour bridge, only her angle was a bit precarious.

She stopped leaning and stood and watched the traffic below. *So* much traffic. She could see the sea if she craned her neck, but she couldn't smell it. All she could smell was traffic fumes.

She was so homesick…

Oh, for heaven's sake, she liked visiting Sydney. She liked the shopping, the restaurants, the anonymity. It was only the fear of the last twenty-four hours that was making her feel bereft.

But it was also the thought of her conversation with Marc. The difficulties of continuing on the island as her grandpa grew older.

She thought of Robert's heart, the risks of returning long-term to the island, the difficulty of coping as the island's only doctor. Even if he wanted to, Robert could hardly continue—she knew that. She'd be on her own.

And with that came a wash of despair so profound that she found she was shaking.

'Oh, cut it out.' She said it out loud, scolding herself. 'You won't be on your own. You'll have all the islanders. And if things get really desperate you can always marry Tony and have a tribe of kids and never feel lonely again.'

Except…loneliness wasn't always about a lack of people. Loneliness was being without a person.

One special person.

Marc?

'Well, you can cut that out too,' she said, even louder. 'You've known the man for what, four days, and here you are fantasising about him…'

'I kind of like fantasising about him.' She was arguing with herself now. 'If I moved to Sydney I might…we might…'

'And ditto for that thought, too.' Her own two-way conversation was getting heated. 'He's a high-flying doctor with high-flying friends. If I moved to Sydney I'd be lucky to get a job in some outer suburban clinic, somewhere cheap enough for us to live, with an increasingly dependent grandpa. There's not the slightest chance there'd be anything between me and Marc.

'But he kissed me.' There it was, a solid fact. She tried to hug it to herself as a promise—and failed.

'So he's a good kisser,' her sane self argued. 'He only kissed me to make me feel better. It's probably quicker and easier for a guy like that to give a decent kiss than to say "I hope you feel better soon".'

Luckily her sense of humour stepped in there to make her grin at the suddenly ridiculous vision of Marc doing ward rounds, kissing everyone as he went.

Like he'd kissed her?

Her fingers moved almost involuntarily to her mouth, as if she could still feel the pressure of his lips. His warmth, his strength, his solid, comforting, sexy, amazing self.

Marc…

'You're behaving like a teenager with a crush,' she told herself harshly, and stared down at the traffic again. 'Me and Marc? You're dreaming. Like me and Grandpa moving to Sydney. No and no and no.'

The thought of Robert dragged her out of her pointless conversation with herself, back to reality. She needed to head back to Intensive Care to see him. He'd be nervous about the upcoming surgery—no, he'd be terrified. She'd need every resource she possessed to calm him.

'So stop thinking about Marc and think about Grandpa.'

'I am thinking about Grandpa,' she said out loud again. 'And I'm thinking about me and the island and a heart specialist with a broken leg who's so far out of my league that I need my head read to be thinking about him. I need to get Grandpa better and then go home. Maybe even to Tony.

'Are you out of your mind? Tony? No!

'Yeah, but five little Tonys might make you happy.

'Buy yourself five dogs,' she snapped to herself. 'Dogs are a much safer bet than people any day.'

CHAPTER ELEVEN

TWELVE DAYS LATER Elsa and Robert flew back to the island on the normal passenger flight. Elsa had told Marc they were coming. He'd had every intention of meeting the plane, but where medicine was concerned plans were made to be broken.

He'd been inundated with minor issues since Boxing Day—sunburn, sunstroke, lacerations, stomach upsets, a couple of kids with alcohol poisoning after drinking their father's high shelf spirits on New Year's Eve. The works.

When Elsa and Robert's plane touched down he was in Theatre, sewing up a lacerated thigh. Bob Cruikshank, the local realtor, had hired tradesmen to construct a cluster of holiday cottages, and progress was slow. In an attempt to hurry things up over the holiday period he'd bought himself a chainsaw to cut planking, with the aim of building the decks himself. It wasn't his brightest idea. That he hadn't bled to death was pure luck. A neighbour had heard his yell and knew enough to apply pressure while calling for help.

'I guess you need training to operate those

things,' Bob had said feebly, as Macka's police van-cum-ambulance had brought him in.

'I imagine chainsaw operation doesn't get included in most realtor training manuals,' Marc agreed. The cut was deep and filthy. He was incredibly lucky he hadn't cut nerves.

Marc would have preferred to use local anaesthetic but Bob was deeply shocked and agitated. It had to be a general anaesthetic, using Maggie to monitor breathing.

It wasn't optimal but it was the only choice. Then, halfway through the procedure, Elsa walked in. 'Hi, guys,' she said as she stood in the doorway. 'Anything I can do to help?'

'Oh, thank heaven,' Maggie said vehemently.

Marc had his forceps on a sliver of wood that was dangerously close to the artery. He couldn't afford to look up. It didn't stop him reacting, though. Elsa was back. Maggie's 'thank heaven' didn't begin to describe the sensation he felt hearing her voice.

His reaction was disproportionate. Undeniable.

'Hooray, you're back,' Maggie was saying. 'Can you take over here? Doc Pierce has been talking me through it, but we're worried about his oxygen levels.' Then she amended the statement. 'No, *Dr Pierce* is worried about Bob's oxygen levels. My job's just to tell him what the monitors are saying and doing what he tells me.'

'They told me out front what's been happening,' Elsa said briefly. 'I've already scrubbed.'

'Then I'm back to being nurse assistant.' Maggie handed over to Elsa, and Marc's stress level dropped about tenfold. He'd been operating at the same time as watching and instructing Maggie. Bob was a big man with background health issues, and the anaesthetic was as fraught as the surgery itself.

The question slammed back, as it had hit him over and over for the past few days. How the hell could Elsa work here alone?

The splinter of wood finally came free. He gave a grunt of satisfaction and glanced up.

'Welcome back,' he said, and smiled. She looked strained, he thought, but she still looked great. Fantastic. Something deep in his gut seemed to clench. It was all he could do not to abandon Bob and go hug her.

'Thank you,' she said primly. 'How's the needlework?'

'Basic.' Somehow he made his voice prosaic. Professional. As if she was a colleague and nothing else. 'If I'd realised how grubby this injury was internally, I'd have had him evacuated. I'm just lucky we didn't try this under local.'

'Bob would never had cooperated under local,' she told him. 'He'd have been demanding to take pictures for his Facebook page and probably fainting in the process.' She hesitated. 'You know he has emphysema?'

'I read his file.' He was starting a final clear and swab before stitching. 'That's why we've gone for the lightest anaesthesia possible. How's your grandpa?'

'Okay. Resting.'

'He should have stayed another week.'

'You try telling him that. He's pig-stubborn.'

'Too pig-stubborn to accept he needs to back right off, workwise?'

'I guess…' She sighed. 'He accepts that.'

'Excellent.' And then he threw out the question which had become a constant drumming in his head as the load of tourist patients had escalated. 'Elsa, how the hell are you going to manage here on your own?'

There was a moment's silence. Too long a silence.

'I'll manage,' she said at last. 'Did I tell you I spent a year's surgery rotation before I came back to the island?' She sounded as if she was struggling for lightness.

'Yeah, but *I* didn't do a year's anaesthetic training.' That was Maggie, entering the conversation with force. She handed Marc a threaded needle and glanced at Elsa with concern. 'Marc's been great, talking me through anaesthetising while he worked, but it's given us both heebie-jeebies. Is Robert going to be well enough to keep this up?'

'I guess. If…if that's all he does.'

'That's not viable and you know it,' Marc growled, thinking of the massive mix of human needs he'd been called on to fill over the past days. 'And you know I'm not just talking about this incident. Elsa, you need help.'

'No other doctor will want to work here with what we can offer.' She said it lightly, as if it didn't matter so much, but he knew it did. 'I need a full-time income, and there's not enough work during non-holiday periods to support two full-time doctors. Not unless we could somehow join the outer islands to form a bigger service, and where would we get the money to do that? We've approached the government before and it's not possible.'

'Then you need to leave,' he said bluntly. 'Maybe offer the job to a couple who might be happy to work here as one and a half doctors.'

'And where would that leave Grandpa and me?' She tilted her chin and met his look head-on. 'It's not your problem, Dr Pierce, so butt out. Right… Are you ready for reverse? You won't want to keep him under for any longer than you need to.'

'Go teach your grandmother to suck eggs,' Marc said, casting her a smile but seeing the strain behind her eyes.

'Sorry… Doctor,' she muttered.

'That's quite all right… Doctor,' he said and tried for another smile. 'And of course you're right to advise me. If you've done a year's surgery rotation and you know the patient you're equipped to give me advice.'

'I'm not sure what I'm equipped for any more,' she said heavily. 'But I suspect I'm about to find out.'

With surgery finished, and with Bob surfacing to hear his wife informing him she'd tossed his chainsaw off a cliff and if he ever lifted so much as a pair of scissors from now on she'd do the same with them, Marc was left with a gap until afternoon clinic. He escaped the escalating row in Bob's room—'Geez, Marjorie, do you know how much that chainsaw cost?'—and limped out to the hospital veranda. He needed to think.

The raised voices of the Cruikshanks followed him. There was little escape on this island, he thought, and then wondered how could Elsa stand it. But she'd been bred into it, he thought. She'd been inculcated with a sense of obligation to the islanders since she was seven. Plus she had her obligation to her grandfather.

But she loved her grandfather. Of course she did. He knew that, but he was on shaky ground here. There wasn't a lot of emotion in his background.

He didn't get the love thing, but somehow that was where his thoughts were heading. The sensation that had overwhelmed him when she'd walked into Theatre had almost blown him away. Was that love? It didn't make sense, and Marc Pierce was a man who liked to make sense of his world.

So make sense of the quandary Elsa has found herself in, he told himself. It was the least he could do.

The least he could do...

Elsa McCrae.

The two collections of words didn't seem to go together.

Elsa was a colleague. She'd saved his life. It made sense to feel gratitude, admiration, obligation. But none of those sentiments accounted for the wave of sensation he'd felt when she'd walked into the theatre just now, and that was troubling him. The way he'd felt then... The way he still felt...

'It's nonsense.' He said the words out loud and Ryan, who tended the hospital garden in between acting as an orderly, raised his head from where he'd been cutting back ferns and looked a query.

'What makes no sense, Doc?'

This dratted island! Was nowhere private? He

hadn't realised Ryan was there. He'd been so caught up in his thoughts.

So say nothing, he told himself. This was his business, not the business of the whole island. Tell Ryan to mind his own.

What came out instead was, 'It makes no sense how two weeks can change your life.'

Ryan rose and scratched filthy fingers on his hat. 'Mate, you can drop dead in two weeks,' he said cheerfully. 'Hey, you might have starved to death in that cave and that wouldn't have even taken two weeks. That would have changed your life and then some.'

'I meant emotionally.' For heaven's sake, what was he doing? He was confessing all to a guy he hardly knew?

But Ryan seemed unperturbed—and also, to Marc's bewilderment, he seemed completely understanding. 'I'm guessing you've fallen for Doc Elsa,' he said simply, as though it was no big deal. 'Well, good luck with that, mate. Every young buck on the island seems to do it at some time. You'll get over it. They all do.'

'Thanks,' he managed weakly, and Ryan gave him a cheery wave and headed off to the compost bin with his wheelbarrow of fern clippings. Leaving his advice behind.

You'll get over it.

It was a sensible statement, the only problem

being that Marc didn't exactly know what *it* was. This thing he was feeling.

It was temporary, he told himself. It was the result of shock and relief and gratitude.

Be practical.

'What you need to do is help her see her way forward,' he said, only this time he said it under his breath because the walls had ears around here.

But that brought another thought. If she did leave the island, if she and Robert moved to Sydney... 'Then maybe we'd have time to...'

And that was where he stopped, because when it came to time to do *what*, he couldn't begin to imagine what that might be.

He should go find a cold shower, he told himself. He should at least talk sense into himself. Instead his thoughts kept drifting to a place that didn't seem at all sensible.

The way he felt about Elsa... The feeling in his gut as she'd walked into Theatre... It seemed a chasm he hadn't even noticed approaching.

So step back. Find solid ground. Accept the way you're feeling and work around it.

'Whatever happens, it'd have to be on my terms,' he said, and this time he said it out loud. He needed to reassure himself there was still room for him to be sensible.

He thought of his gorgeous harbourside house,

inherited from his father, who'd died a few years ago. He thought of the space, the garden, the room for people to live pretty much separately.

'Even if we...' he started to say, but then he paused. He hadn't the least idea where his thoughts were headed.

Even as a child he'd known emotional ties were transitory and he'd never really considered the idea of a permanent relationship. When his friends fell in love he always felt as if he was looking at something totally foreign to him. But with Elsa suddenly his mind was going there whether he willed it or not.

'But my life wouldn't have to change all that much.'

Something at the back of his mind was suddenly flabbergasted. He almost felt dizzy.

'What the hell are you thinking?' he demanded, out loud again, and quickly looked around to make sure Ryan hadn't returned.

He hadn't. He was free to argue with himself.

'I have no idea,' he confessed to the sensible part of his brain, but sensible wasn't winning right now.

Nothing was winning. He kept sitting there. He needed to get his head clear. He needed a plan.

It didn't happen. The dizziness stayed.

Finally he shook his head and limped back into the hospital. He needed something to do. Something medical. Something that had nothing to do with the weird infighting that was going on in his head.

Elsa stayed busy for the rest of the day. Marc had insisted on continuing with the afternoon clinic so she wasn't needed there. She bossed her grandfather into settling down to rest, starting what she hoped would be the new norm. Then she did a round of the hospital patients. Maggie filled her in as she went.

'Marc's been pretty much over everything,' she told her. 'The islanders think he's great. Dotty Morrison has run out of scripts four times—I think she's fallen in love with him.'

'Who wouldn't?' Elsa said absently. She was reading a patient file as she spoke, and was aware of a sudden silence. She glanced up to see that Maggie was skewering her with a look.

'Yeah?' Maggie said softly. 'Really?'

'I just meant…' Elsa flushed. 'Oh, Maggie, cut it out. He's tall, dark and dishy, he saved Grandpa's life, he's taken over my workload and I'm incredibly grateful. What's not to like?'

'The word though,' Maggie said thoughtfully, 'was love.'

'As if that's going to happen.' She let the clip on the file she was reading close with a snap. 'I imagine he'll be leaving tomorrow now I'm back.'

'But you...'

'Oh, for heaven's sake, Maggie, please don't.' To her horror she found she was suddenly close to tears. She closed her eyes and her friend was right there, giving her a hug.

'Hey, Elsa, sweetheart...'

'It's okay.' She let herself savour her friend's hug for a moment and then pulled away, gathering herself together. 'This is just a reaction. From homecoming. From worry about Grandpa.'

'Nothing at all to do with Marc?'

'Maybe,' she admitted. 'But surely I'm allowed to have the same sort of crush that Dottie has? It's been a long couple of weeks and I'm overwrought. Marc's been great and I've let myself fantasise a little. There's nothing else to it.'

'No,' Maggie said thoughtfully. 'Of course there's nothing else. That'd require you putting yourself before the island, maybe even before your grandpa. As if that'd ever happen.'

'And it'd require interest on his part.' It was a snap, and she caught herself. She'd spent twelve stressful days in Sydney trying to figure out her future. What she didn't need now was her friend imagining a non-existent romantic interest to complicate things even further.

'You know, Tony's started to go out with Kylie from the bakery,' Maggie told her, still thoughtful. 'He's obviously given up on you.'

'Bully for Tony.'

'So who else is in the offing?'

'There's no one,' she replied before she could help herself.

'Then why not do a little more than fantasising? Marc's here and he's lovely and he's not attached. He's just split up with his girlfriend and…'

'Have you been grilling him?'

'Of course,' Maggie said, grinning. 'Why not? So the field is clear. Why not go for it?'

'Because he's going back to Sydney and my life is here.'

'Your life might not be able to be here much longer. You need to face facts, love.'

'But not now,' Elsa said with a weary sigh. 'Leave it, Maggie. There are so many complications in my life anyway. Where would I find time for romance?'

'What's wrong with tonight? He's here. He's available. If I was twenty years younger I'd go for it.'

'Maggie!'

'Chicken.'

'I'd rather be a chicken than a dead hen.'

'And I'd rather have a wild fling with a gorgeous doctor than be a chicken,' Maggie said, and chuckled and headed back to the wards.

Elsa was left floundering. A wild fling? She'd never had such a thing. He'd be gone in the next couple of days. How could she possibly expose her heart like that?

She headed through to her house, adjoining the hospital. The locals had been in as soon as they'd learned she and Robert were home, and casseroles and cakes were lined up on the bench.

The islanders had helped her for ever, she thought as she sorted them. They'd supported her grandpa in raising her. They'd helped cover the cost of her medical training.

A wild fling? She thought of Maggie's words and rejected them. A fling and then what? It'd leave her unhappy, unsettled, ungrateful for the life she needed to live.

'At least I'll never go hungry *if* I stay here,' she told Sherlock—who was already looking tubbier after two weeks of islander care—and heard the *if* that she'd just said.

Ouch.

Robert was asleep. She roused him. They ate one of the casseroles together but he was silent throughout, and then he headed straight back to bed. The last few days seemed to have aged him ten years or more.

She washed and wiped, then let Sherlock out. There was a brief bark and she thought there must be a possum on the veranda. She should chase it off to protect her grapevines and then she thought, *Who cares about grapevines?*

She felt totally, absolutely discombobulated. Then she walked outside, and if it was possible to feel even more discombobulated, she did.

Marc was sitting on the back step, under the outside light. Just sitting.

'Marc!'

'Hey,' he said, rising and backing away a little. 'It's only me. I know this looks like stalking, but I didn't want to interrupt you and your grandpa. We need to talk, so I thought—what would I do if I'd been off this island for twelve days? I'd want to soak it up, that's what. So I decided to come here and wait.'

She eyed him with suspicion that was definitely justified. 'So you just guessed where I might be?' she ventured. 'It wasn't Maggie who told you I mostly drink a glass of wine out on my back step after dinner?'

'Okay, it might have been,' he confessed, and he sent her a lopsided smile that did something to her heart that she somehow had to ignore. He motioned to a bottle and two glasses set out on the top step. 'I brought these. Just in case.'

She harrumphed her indignation at her scheming friend. 'I don't believe Maggie.'

'She's great.'

'She's incorrigible.'

'But she's still great.'

'Yeah,' she said, casting him another suspicious glare, but then she succumbed. This was her porch after all, and there was wine. She plonked herself down on the top step and filled a glass and then filled one for him. 'Everyone's great. I have seventeen casseroles jammed into the freezer, that's how great everyone is. I won't have to cook for a month.'

'Lucky you.' He sat down beside her. Not too close. Still giving her space. Sherlock, glorying in having his mistress back, but also extremely pleased to see his new friend, wriggled in between them.

Silence. The warmth of the night closed over them. The surf below the house provided the faint hush of waves. The moon had flung a ribbon of silver out over the water. A bush turkey was scratching somewhere in the bushes—she could hear its faint rustle.

This man had her so off-balance. The concerns that had been building over the last twelve days were still with her.

Marc's presence here tonight wasn't helping a bit.

It was Marc who finally broke the silence. 'Elsa, I've been thinking,' he told her. 'I came to tell you I can take another two weeks off before I need to return to Sydney. You don't need to jump back into work straight away. Give yourself some space. Your grandpa needs you.'

'Everyone needs me.' It was said flatly, an inescapable fact.

There was another moment's silence. And then, 'You know,' Marc said softly into the stillness, 'I could get to need you, too.'

And with that, all the complications of the islanders' needs, her grandfather's needs, fell away. There was so much in Marc's statement it took her breath away.

She sat with her wine glass in her hand, but she could well have dropped it. She was looking out to sea but seeing nothing. There was some sort of fog in her mind. Some dense mist that meant she couldn't make sense of what he'd just said.

She didn't want to make sense of it?

'I… That's not very helpful,' she said at last because, for some stupid reason, the first thing that came into her head wasn't rejection. It was simply impossibility.

In answer he lifted the glass from her suddenly limp hand and set it aside. Then he took her hand in his. He didn't tug her to face him, though. He simply intertwined their fingers and let the silence envelop them again.

His hand was strong. Warm. Compelling.

Impossible.

The word was slamming round and round her head, like a metal ball bashing against the sides as it bounced. It hurt.

'Elsa, you can't continue to do this alone,' he said softly at last. 'You know you can't. I've been talking to Maggie. She says you were barely managing before Robert had this attack. She said the walk you went on when you found me was the first time you'd taken time off for weeks.'

'What's that got to do...'

'With you and me? Nothing,' he told her. 'Except everything.'

'You're not offering to come here and help, are you?'

'I'd love to say I would, but no. I'm a cardiologist, not a family doctor. I need to go where my skills are most needed. In two weeks we have new interns starting rotation at the hospital, so I need to be back in Sydney.'

'Two weeks' medical help would be great,' she told him, struggling desperately to sound practical. 'But where does that fit with what you're saying about need?'

'I'm talking of possibilities in the future.' He spread his hands. 'Elsa, I come from a background that's emotionally barren, to say the least. My parents were rich and dysfunctional, and they used money as a substitute for affection. The way I feel about you has me confused. Blindsided, if you like. You and me...'

'There is no you and me.'

'There might be. I have no idea, but the way I'm feeling…isn't it worth exploring?'

She was well out of her comfort zone now, feeling as if she were swimming in uncharted waters, towards what seemed like a whirlpool.

'The way you're feeling?' She intended her voice to sound mocking, but she was mocking herself as well as him. There was no choice but to mock the impossibility of what he was saying. 'You've known me for what, four days?'

'We've talked every day while you were in Sydney.'

They had. Every night after Robert slept she'd rung him, ostensibly to check if there were any medical problems on the island. Which she knew there weren't. Or he'd rung to consult on something she knew he didn't really need to consult with her about. In the end they'd abandoned reasons and simply talked. She'd sat on her balcony in her anonymous hospital relatives' apartment and she'd talked to him as a friend.

Only now he felt like more than a friend.

When had that line been crossed?

It hadn't, she told herself frantically. It couldn't. She needed to get a grip.

'Marc, what we're both feeling… It's just that we've both been thrown into fraught situations,' she managed. 'I've been frightened and stressed, and you've been a godsend. You came here for hours, with plans to head off for a glamorous holiday, with glamorous friends…a glamorous girlfriend.'

'And found a friend who's maybe not so glamorous,' he said seriously. 'But a friend who's beautiful. Who's caring, brave, funny, devoted…'

'To my island. To my people.'

'There's a complication.'

'You think?' She almost snapped it at him. 'If this really was…a thing…'

'It's interesting, this thing,' he said, and his eyes were smiling. Oh, that smile… 'We can't define it. To be honest, I'm all at sea with what I'm feeling, yet maybe I know what it might be.'

'Well, it can't be,' she said. 'And if it is…' She struggled to find a way to say what she had no words for. 'If this…thing…turns out to be, I don't know, more than just a passing thing, then where would we go from there?'

'Anywhere you like.'

'Like that's possible.' Anger came to her aid then, and it helped. 'You work in one of the most prestigious coronary care units in the world. I work on this island.'

'But you need to leave.' His words were gentle enough, but behind them she heard a note of implacability. 'Elsa, you know this island needs more than one doctor, and your grandpa can't keep working. I know the island will hardly support another doctor who needs a full wage, but there are medical couples who might well jump at the lifestyle. Couples who'd like the opportunity for one to work part-time. For the island's sake, Elsa, you need to open up that opportunity.'

'By leaving?'

'By leaving.' It was said flatly. A truth that hurt.

'But how do I know any other doctor would give my islanders the care they deserve?' She'd thought this through—of course she had. She'd spent a long time in Sydney contemplating her future. 'What if some nine-to-fiver takes over? Where would my island be then? So what's the choice? If I leave here and make Grandpa safer, the islanders would be at risk and Grandpa would be deeply unhappy. If I stay here I need to accept that Grandpa will probably die earlier. But Grandpa and I have discussed it and it's no choice at all. He wants to stay.'

'So where does that leave you personally? Or... us?' His eyes were still on hers, serious, questioning. 'Maybe that's what we need to find out.'

'I don't understand.'

'I think you do. This thing we're feeling...'

'I don't want...' But her voice trailed off. She didn't want what? A nebulous something. A problem that had no solution?

This man?

All of him was compelling, she thought. He was drawing her into some sweet web she had no hope of escaping. But it was a web she had to escape, because her grandfather's happiness, the security of the islanders, depended on it.

'Marc...'

'You know, I don't understand it either,' he said, and there was a note of uncertainty in his voice that told her he was speaking the truth. 'Honestly, Elsa, I didn't expect to feel like this about someone so...'

'Unsuitable,' she finished for him, but he shook his head.

'You know that's not true. But different, yes. I've been brought up without family ties. My father was indifferent to his family, committed to his work. My mother was loyal in her own way—sort of—but her work and the mountains always came first. I was essentially raised by servants. But the way you feel about your grandpa...'

'It's normal.'

'It's great.'

'It's no big deal. It's just called love.'

'I get that. It's just... I didn't think I could feel...'

'Well, don't feel,' she said, breathless now but angry again. What was he doing, sitting on her back step looking like he was offering her the world when she knew very well that the world wasn't his to offer? Her tiny part of the world was prescribed, definite, and there was no escape clause.

'I don't think this thing is something that can be turned off at will,' he was saying.

'Then put a plug in it. Take your wine and go back to your side of the hospital.' While she was away he'd shifted out of his hospital bed and was staying in an apartment used for the occasional patient relative who needed to stay overnight.

'I will—in a moment. Elsa, I'm not threatening you.'

'But you are. My life can't change. I have no choice.'

'You have no choice but to change.'

'But not with you.'

'Elsa.' He reached out and caught both her hands, compelling now, assured. 'You sound terrified but there's no need. I'm not threatening,' he repeated.

'You are.'

'Is it me you're frightened of or the situation?'

There was no answer to that. She tried to sort it in her head, but her head was struggling to co-operate. Was she frightened of her situation? Being forced to leave the island to make her living somewhere else? Was she terrified of breaking her grandfather's heart by insisting he leave the island, too? Yes, she was.

Was she frightened of Marc? No, but she was frightened of the way she was feeling.

He was being practical whereas she…

She was totally, absolutely terrified, because falling for this man, exposing what she wanted most in all the world seemed unthinkable.

'Elsa, relax,' Marc said, gently now, as he watched her face. 'Stop it with the convolutions. Just feel.'

Just feel. So easy for him to say. But his hands were holding hers. His eyes were holding hers too, and what she saw there… She managed to fight back panic just for a moment, and in that moment something else surged in. Something sweet and sure and right. Something strong enough to drive everything else from her tired mind.

Love? Who knew? All she knew was that suddenly she was over trying to understand what she felt. He was sitting beside her in the moonlight, turned towards her. His eyes were gentle, kind and he was tugging her close.

She should protest. She should pull away. She should do a million things.

She didn't. The night seemed to dissolve. Everything melted away as his hands tugged her closer. As he released her for a nanosecond so that instead of holding her hands he was cupping her face. Tilting her chin. Looking into her eyes, searching for a truth she didn't understand.

The fight, the logic had simply disappeared.

Almost of their own volition, her arms moved to hold him, and with that hold came surety, strength, power. In the last few days her world had been tilting so much that at times she'd felt in danger of falling off.

This man was no long-term safe anchorage—she knew that—but for now he was here, he was Marc, and he was holding her.

He wanted her and she wanted him. Nothing more, nothing less.

He was holding her, but he'd paused, a fraction of a breath away from kissing her. This was no practised seduction. The final decision was being left to her.

And with that knowledge came a longing so strong, so fierce that any reservations disappeared into the night.

He was giving her space but she wanted no space.

'Yes,' she murmured. She hardly knew whether the word was said out loud or not, but there was room for no other.

His mouth claimed hers, and the way she was feeling there'd be no need for words for ever.

What was he doing?

He knew damned well what he was doing. He

was kissing a woman he wanted in a way he'd never wanted a woman before.

To have and to hold… He'd heard those lines before, in the marriage ceremonies of countless friends, but until now they'd simply been a formality.

They weren't a formality. *To have and to hold.* That was what he wanted, what he was melting into—a sense of rightness…desire. Possession?

She was in his arms and she felt as if she belonged. She did belong there. This was his woman and as his mouth claimed her, so did his head.

Elsa. *His woman.*

She was letting him kiss her, and unbelievably she was kissing him back. The desire between them was white-hot, a fire that felt all-consuming.

The porch light was on. They could probably be seen by half the island—and indeed Sherlock had backed away and was watching them, his head cocked to one side as if this was a moment he should take note of. It was merely a kiss, but it felt like much, much more.

It felt like a joining. A claiming. It was a sensation of being where he belonged. Home? Who knew what such a word meant, but it suddenly seemed like a siren song.

And when they finally pulled apart, as pull apart they were forced to do because Sherlock finally decided what they were doing seemed interesting and he might just join in, Marc knew his world had changed.

'Elsa…' The word was a caress. She was looking at him in confusion. Her hands were cupping her cheeks and a blush of rose had spread across her face.

'I don't…'

'Don't understand? Neither do I.' He went to take her hands again, but she pulled back. As he watched he saw her confusion turning to fear.

'Marc, don't.'

'You don't want this?'

'Yes. No! I can't.'

'Why not, my love?' Was this the first time he'd ever used such an endearment? No matter, it felt right.

But the look of fear was still there. 'Marc, I can't afford to fall in love with you.'

'Hey, I'm cheap to run,' he told her, trying to take the fear from her face. Trying to make light of what seemed so important. 'In fact, I might even run in the black rather than the red. I make a decent income as a cardiologist, you know, and I'm wealthy in my own right.'

She tried to laugh but it didn't happen. It turned into a choke that seemed perilously close to a sob.

'As if that matters. Marc, this can't happen. It's far too soon.'

'Well, *too soon* is something we can do something about,' he told her. 'We have all the time in the world to sort out *too soon*.'

'You're going back to Sydney.'

'Which is where I think you should go, too. I have friends, influence… Love, there'll be a score of jobs for a doctor with your skills. You'll find work in a minute. My house is huge and you're welcome to stay there, but if it's indeed *too soon* then we can find you and Robert a decent apartment while we figure how long is soon enough.' Then he glanced at Sherlock who was looking at him in confusion. 'Or,' he added practically, 'a house with a backyard.'

'So Sherlock can stay in the backyard all day and Grandpa can stay in the house?'

'Your grandpa will die if he stays on the island,' he said bluntly. 'You've seen the cardiology reports and the reports from the renal physician. He needs constant monitoring. That heart of his is no longer strong enough to cope with anything worse than a bad cold.'

'You don't know that.'

'I can guess it, and so can you.'

'Then it's Grandpa's choice.' Her hands were still holding her cheeks. She looked stressed, frightened—but also angry. 'Marc, why are you saying this? It has to be our decision, mine and Grandpa's, where we live, and our choice is here.'

'Then we'll never see how our relationship might work.'

'That's blackmail!'

'It's only blackmail if you want what I think we both want. To see if you and I...'

'There is no you and I.' The anger was still there. 'There can't be a *you and I* unless you decide that being an islander is part of your life plan. But people don't come here to live. They're born here, and some of them stay and some of them don't. Apart from half a dozen hippies who live at the far end of the island where the surf's best, no one's migrated here for decades.'

'I know that, which is why...'

'Which is why I have to leave if I want a life with anyone other than another islander. But that's okay because my other islander is my grandpa.'

'He won't live for ever.'

'So you're threatening me as well as blackmailing me?'

'Elsa...'

'Leave it.' She closed her eyes for a moment and when she opened them again he saw a wash of weariness so deep it was all he could do not to reach out and support her. But she was holding out her hands in a gesture that said she was warding him off, not wanting him to come closer.

He'd stuffed it.

He'd totally, absolutely stuffed it.

He'd only spoken the truth.

But it hadn't worked. She was tipping the untouched wine from her glass onto the garden. She was done.

'Go back to your quarters, Marc,' she said quietly. 'I have enough to think about tonight without a proposal that has so many impossible conditions that it makes me feel ill.'

'It wasn't a proposal,' he denied automatically. Or was it? The way he'd framed it…

'Then I'm glad,' she said, and sighed and clicked her fingers. Sherlock sidled to her side, cocking his head to one side as if he was trying to figure what was wrong. Then he nuzzled next to her leg and pressed his body against her knee. It was an unmistakable gesture of comfort, and Marc looked down at the dog and thought that Sherlock had got it right.

And he'd got it impossibly wrong.

'I'll still stay for two weeks anyway,' he told her, searching for anything to allay the pain he could feel washing over her in waves. 'That should take care of the worst of the tourist season.'

'Thank you,' she said simply. 'We'll pay you full time clinician rates.'

'There's no need…'

'There's every need,' she said, suddenly angry again. 'From now on… Well, we'll start as we mean to go on, Dr Pierce. As medical colleagues and nothing more.'

CHAPTER TWELVE

MARC HAD TWO weeks to repair the mistakes of that night. He had two weeks to find a way to undo the damage.

In two weeks he found not a single solution.

She was pig stubborn, he told himself as it neared the time he had to leave. She had to face a future off the island.

And yet, as he saw Robert gradually regain health, as he watched the elderly doctor sitting on the veranda with Sherlock at his feet, with his islander mates sitting beside him, as he saw Robert's devotion to the islanders and the islanders' devotion to Robert, he had to concede that it'd be extremely hard to drag him to a new life in Sydney.

Yet it meant that Elsa could have no new life. Until…

Yeah, that was a good thing to think—not. Wait until her grandfather died to move away? How bleak was that? But meanwhile, for Elsa to work herself into the ground holding this practice together while she waited for her grandfather's health to fail, as it surely must without specialist care…

It made him feel ill to imagine it, but there was nothing he could do.

He worked beside her, taking clinics while she did house calls and took care of the patients in the hospital. That had been pretty much the set-up before Robert fell ill, and it worked. The island could function on one and a half doctors, but that doctor couldn't be Robert.

Nor could it be Marc. He'd thought of staying on the island—of course he had—but he wasn't so deeply thrown by these new emotions that he failed to see the impossibility of such a plan. He was a cardiologist and there was little here for him to do. He'd worked hard to achieve his skill set. Managing the occasional imperative heart problem on Gannet with no support staff… No.

But the more he saw of Elsa, the more he knew how much he wanted her. He also knew how badly he'd messed up his proposal. Blackmail and threats? It honestly hadn't seemed like that to him—surely he'd only been laying out the truth—but he knew he'd hurt her.

And that hurt him. As he saw her flinch whenever she caught sight of him in the distance, as he saw each flash of pain in her eyes, as he watched her quickly turn away, he knew his clumsy attempts to get her to accept a future off the island had done nothing but cause her distress. He felt gutted.

So what to do?

There was little he could do. He worked on. Elsa paid him and he couldn't refuse—she said she'd lock the clinic doors on him if he didn't accept it. He funnelled the payments via Maggie into funds for a new incubator, something the hospital desperately needed.

'I'll tell Elsa it's from an anonymous donor,' Maggie said when he proposed it. 'She might suspect it's from you, but she doesn't need to know for sure. If she did…well, she's already grateful to you for the lift chairs and this might stress her more.'

'Because?'

'You know very well why,' she said, irritated. But then she softened. 'I know it's an impossible situation and I'm desperately sorry that the pair of you can't take this further, but this is our Elsa we're talking about. Ours.'

Ours. The island's.

That line wormed its way back into his head. *To have and to hold.*

The island had staked its claim and it was holding on. Elsa was staying, and the bottom line was that he had to leave.

So he worked on, but as he did he racked his brain as to how he could help her. Half a doctor—

that was what she needed. That was what Gannet Island needed. It couldn't be him, not long-term, but she had to have help.

None of his colleagues would be even vaguely interested. They were all high-flying achievers.

So where to find half a doctor?

And then, a week before he was due to leave, he found himself thinking of his mother, mixing medicine with mountain climbing.

Half a doctor...

He started making phone calls. Half a doctor couldn't be him, but at least this could help Elsa.

It wasn't nearly enough, he thought as his departure date loomed closer, but at least it was something.

It seemed *something* was all he had left to offer.

Saturday. The day of his flight home. He'd asked Elsa to have dinner with him on Friday night and she'd agreed—'But at our kitchen table with Grandpa. We still have a mountain of casseroles.'

What followed was a stilted dinner where he and Robert talked medicine and island history, and Elsa said little at all. She saw him to the door afterwards and he wanted to kiss her—no, he was desperate to kiss her—but she backed away. The closed look on her face said there was no compromise. Ryan drove him to the airport the next morning, and that was that.

But then, just as the incoming plane landed, he saw Elsa's car pull into the car park. He watched and waited, saw her hesitate as if she was regretting coming and wasn't too sure she was doing the right thing, but then she came right in.

This was a tiny airport. There weren't such things as separate arrival and departure lounges. She walked through the swing doors and saw him straight away.

'Hey,' he said as she reached him. Her eyes were troubled. Sad. He desperately wanted to hug her, but somehow he stopped himself and managed to smile. 'Going somewhere?'

She tried to smile back. 'You must know that I wish I could.'

He did know that. It was breaking something inside him, but he understood.

'I just… I couldn't let you go before I thanked you again,' she told him. 'Last night was too formal. Too…unhappy. I didn't say it, just how grateful Grandpa and I are for all you've done.'

'You don't need to say it,' he told her. 'The thanks on both sides just about balance themselves out. And I've brought you trouble. I'm so sorry, Elsa, that I've made you feel…'

'Trapped?' she told him and managed a smile. 'That's not your call. I felt trapped long before you arrived.'

'But you still won't come to Sydney.'

'Don't go there again, Marc. You know it's impossible. I'd still be trapped in Sydney, only it'd be worse. I'd have an unhappy Grandpa and I'd have the islanders on my mind for the rest of my life.'

You'd have me. He wanted to say it, but he couldn't. The time for that was over.

'So I just need to say goodbye,' she told him, and she reached out and took his hands. Around them a small group of his fellow travellers were doing much the same, hugging goodbye, shaking hands, shedding tears.

That was how he felt. Like shedding tears. How could he feel like this about a woman he'd known for such a short time?

How could he feel like this about any woman?

No woman but Elsa.

'Goodbye, Marc,' she told him and the tug on his hands was suddenly urgent. She pulled him close and then reached up and kissed him.

It was a light kiss, a feather touch. A friends' farewell.

Good friends. Friends who could never be more.

His instinct was to kiss her back, tug her arms around him… *To have and to hold.*

He couldn't. He didn't. She stepped back and he let her go.

'Marc!' It was a booming yell from the far side

of the lounge, where a cluster of incoming passengers were collecting their baggage.

He turned and saw a woman, middle-aged, small and dumpy, dressed for what looked like a two-week hike. She'd just gathered a gigantic pack from the pile of baggage and was hitching it onto her back as she yelled.

'Stella,' he said and then grinned. Of course it was Stella. He'd thought she wouldn't get here for days, yet here she was.

She was stumping her way towards him. With the pack she was carrying she was almost as wide as she was high.

'I'll go,' Elsa said quickly but he caught her hand.

'No. I'm glad this has happened. This is someone I'd like you to meet.'

'Marc,' the woman said again as she reached them and she gripped his hand with a ferocity that made him wince. 'Excellent,' she boomed. 'A handover. How long do we have before the plane leaves?'

'Only minutes,' he told her, 'but Elsa can fill you in.' He turned to Elsa, who was looking faintly stunned. 'Elsa, this is Stella Harbour—Dr Harbour. Stella, this is Dr McCrae. Elsa, Stella's a hiking friend of my mother's. She retired from family medicine a couple of years ago and has been hiking the world since.'

'And starting to get bored doing it,' Stella said bluntly. 'Not that I haven't seen some amazing places, but Marc's call seemed a godsend. I'm missing my medicine. Not that it's a sure thing,' she said hastily, seeing Elsa's look of incomprehension. 'I'm here to hike all over this island, and while I'm doing it I'll be seeing if there might be a place here for me. A work place, I mean.'

'What...?' Elsa managed.

'He didn't tell you? No, he said he'd leave it up to me to explain. Now, you don't have to have me if you don't want me. Marc was clear on that. He said there might be the possibility of work that'd fluctuate according to need. Not much in the quiet times, but full-on in the peak of the tourist season. Which pretty much suits me beautifully. I don't depend on work to provide an income. I love this island—Marc's mum and I hiked here together a couple of times. Peak tourist times are the times when I hate being on the trails anyway and I'd far rather be sewing up cuts and being busy. Anyway, no decision needed yet, my dear. Marc just put it forward as an option, so I thought I'd come over, do a couple of hikes and maybe see if you could make use of me.'

Elsa stared at her as if she couldn't believe what she was seeing—and then she turned to Marc. 'How...?'

'I thought laterally,' he said, smiling at the

confusion—and hope—he saw on her face. 'I remembered the host of lady bushwalkers my mother collected around her, thought of their demographic—pretty much all nearing retiring age—so I rang Mum's best friend.'

'And Lucy rang round all of us with a medical background—there were a few because you know Marc's mum was a medical researcher? And when Lucy rang me... Well, it sounds perfect. To live and work here...'

'I need to go now,' Marc said apologetically. The boarding call for his flight was getting insistent. 'Elsa, Stella knows this is an idea only. If you don't like it then...'

'Then I get a walking holiday here, and no one's the worse off,' Stella added cheerfully. 'Of you go, dear,' she told Marc and gave him a gentle push. 'Back to your cardiology and leave the nuts and bolts of general medicine to us. Byee.'

'Marc...' Elsa said helplessly.

'Do what's best for you,' Marc told her. He hoisted his bag over his shoulder, found his balance on his still-plastered leg and looked at her for one last time. 'Goodbye, Elsa.'

'Marc,' she said again, and then, before he could anticipate what she intended, she reached up and cupped his face and tugged it down to hers.

And kissed him. Fiercely. Possessively.

And then she let him go with a gasp that turned into something that was suspiciously like a sob.

But it was cut off. She put a hand to her face as if to hide her emotions, and when her hand dropped again she had herself under control.

'Goodbye, Marc,' she said and somehow she managed it without so much as a tremor. 'Thank you and farewell.'

He sat on the plane, looking out on the island receding in the distance below and felt blank. Empty. Done.

His leg ached. Everything ached.

Work was piling up in Sydney. He had interns starting on Monday. He had a paper to present at a conference in New York at the beginning of next month. He had a meeting this week with researchers investigating a new drug that promised to reduce blood pressure without the current side-effects.

His diary also showed a party next Saturday that sounded amazing—Grant Thurgood's fortieth would surely be the social event of the season. Grant was a cardiologist at the top of his game, his wife was a socialite extraordinaire and the money and effort they'd thrown at this event would take their guests' collective breath away.

He tried to imagine Elsa throwing such a party,

and couldn't. He tried to imagine Elsa living in that milieu, and couldn't.

Unbidden, his hands moved to his face. To his mouth. As if he could still taste her.

Elsa.

He glanced down at the island beneath him. Somewhere down there Elsa would be talking to Stella, planning a future. Without him.

That was okay. It had to be. Solitude had been pretty much drilled into him from childhood, and it was the easy retreat now.

Life would move on, he told himself. No matter what Elsa decided, it was hardly his business now. He'd thought of marriage when he'd suggested she move to Sydney, but honestly...would he be any good at it?

Elsa would be good at it, he thought. Loving was her specialty, but she surely deserved better than him.

But the pressure from that kiss was still with him and it wouldn't leave. Maybe solitude wasn't so appealing.

But maybe... nothing. Was he still thinking about marriage? If she couldn't leave the island it was impossible to go down that road unless he joined her, abandoned his career, became a part-time generalist.

But that thought was rejected almost before it was formed. He didn't have the empathy, the skills, to be a really good family doctor. A month of such medicine had left him in awe of what Elsa did, but he'd also accepted she had a skill set that was just as important as any cardiology techniques he'd learned. He'd go crazy, watching Elsa seamlessly do what he couldn't. He had to have a challenge.

A challenge… The word seemed to hang.

From up here he could see all the islands, the six that made up the Birding group. He'd seen patients from the outer isles while he'd been at Gannet. He'd even visited a couple, with their remote medical clinics run by capable nurses.

Six islands.

They were Elsa's responsibility. Not his.

Why did it seem as if they were his?

He'd booked a double seat so he could stretch his leg. That meant he was undisturbed, so now he sat back and closed his eyes. Forcing his mind to go blank was a technique he used when he was struggling to find a solution to a fraught medical dilemma—clear all preconceived ideas and start from scratch.

This was surely a dilemma. He needed his technique now.

And suddenly it worked. His mind switched into overdrive and fragments were shooting at him like brightly lit arrows from all sides.

Six islands.

A career that was challenging.

Stella and her mountain climbing and part-time medicine.

Part-time doctors.

A jigsaw that could be put together?

Maybe.

The jumble was coalescing into a whole that was making him feel dizzy.

'It'll never work,' he said out loud, and the flight attendant was suddenly at his side, looking concerned. She was being super helpful to someone she obviously saw as disabled.

'Sir? Is there something wrong?'

She was middle-aged, friendly, reminding him of Maggie. She smiled encouragingly, and amazingly he found himself talking.

'Just a problem I'm trying to solve.'

'Is there anything I can do to help?' The plane was half empty. Clearly she had time to chat.

'I don't think anything's wrong,' he said slowly. 'Except... I might just need to toss my job.'

'Oh, but surely your leg will get better.' She still sounded worried. 'This is the only plane that services Gannet so we know all about you. You were trapped underground. That must have been an awful experience, but surely your life can get back to normal now.'

'But maybe it wasn't being trapped that stopped

me feeling normal.' He was feeling as confused as she was looking. 'Maybe it was being rescued.'

'I gather it was Dr McCrae who found you,' the woman said, and smiled encouragingly. 'She has quite a reputation among the islanders. She'd have kept you safe if anyone could. The islanders think she's wonderful.'

'She is indeed,' Marc said softly.

'Well, take care of yourself, sir.' Duty done, she left to check on the other passengers and Marc was left with his circling thoughts. Which centred now around Elsa.

He let his mind drift back to that time of being trapped with Elsa. Her warmth. Her humour. The feeling that he was safe with her.

And then later… The way she'd melted into him as he'd kissed her. The feeling that he'd found his way home.

Home?

Home was Sydney. Home was a demanding clinical life, his research, cutting-edge medicine, friends who felt the same as he did.

As a lone kid of wealthy but dysfunctional parents, his studies and his career had become his refuge. They were still his pole stars. His career and his research were the most important thing, and everything else fitted around the edges.

What if home was the pole star?

'You need two pole stars,' he said out loud.

He'd read that in an astronomy encyclopaedia his father had given him when he was seven.

Earth's pole stars are Polaris, a magnitude two star aligned approximately with its northern axis, and Polaris Australis, a much dimmer star...

The book had been a birthday gift when he was seven. His parents had been shouting at each other before he'd even unwrapped it, and afterwards they'd been rigidly formal, bidding him goodnight with their anger still obvious.

He'd buried himself in the pole stars. Two pole stars used for navigation for thousands of years.

Pole stars guiding him home. There was that word again.

Home.

Elsa.

He was thinking laterally now. His father's gift of the astronomy book made him think of Elsa's gifts. Her carefully nurtured geraniums. Gifts given with love.

And now he was remembering again the line that had come into his head as he'd held her and kissed her.

To have and to hold.

He couldn't hold her. What sort of arrogance had made him demand that? He wanted to hold

Elsa, but she wouldn't be held just because that was what he wanted.

He wanted to have, but Elsa needed to have as well. She wanted her island. She needed her island.

And there suddenly was his idea, his light bulb moment. His astounding plan.

He thought of his salary. His inherited wealth. His skills, his contacts, his resources. If he couldn't do it, no one could.

It might be impossible, but his light bulb plan was coalescing by the second.

'I won't know unless I try,' he said out loud. He saw the passenger across the aisle eye him with caution, and he grinned. Maybe the guy thought he was nuts and maybe he was. What he was hoping for probably made no sense at all.

'It's politics and funding and feet on the ground,' he muttered. 'And realistically... It'll take at least a year to organise, if it's even possible.'

A year without Elsa? He wanted to turn the plane around now, share his idea with her, tug her into his arms.

To have and to hold? No. Because if it failed, or if he failed... It wasn't fair to either of them.

'A year,' he told himself. A year to change. A whole dammed year.

'You can contact her. Phone her. Go visit her. Be a friend.'

A friend. Friend with benefits?

'As if that's likely to happen. What if she meets someone else? What if she hooks up with that Tony guy?

'It's a risk.' He struggled with the thought, but common sense had to prevail. 'If this is real, if she feels like I do…' He sighed. 'Back off, Pierce, and get your ducks in order first. She's worth fighting for. She's worth risking all. Prove to yourself that you love her enough to wait.'

Love… There was the biggie. Could he really love?

'If you love her then you'll do what it takes,' he told himself. 'Fight for what *she* wants, not for what *you* want. Starting now.'

But still he hesitated, staring out of the window as if he could still see the islands. The urge to turn around and head back to her was overwhelming. Maybe he could do this from Gannet?

He knew he couldn't. He needed to be in Sydney. He needed to be networking, politicking, fighting for something more important than both of them.

'And if I tell her my plan and it fails, then I'll break her heart,' he said out loud. 'But by next Christmas…'

Eleven months. Was it possible?

He turned from the window and flicked open the memo function on his phone to write the first hopeful outline. He was suddenly a man with a purpose. A man with a woman worth fighting for.

'If Elsa can produce a black geranium then surely I can produce a dream,' he vowed. 'But dreams aren't real…

'And neither's Santa Claus,' he told himself. 'But by next Christmas… It's the season of miracles after all, so at least I can try.'

CHAPTER THIRTEEN

Christmas Day, eleven months later:

MARC STARED DOWN at the mountainous Birding
Isles, set in a ring against the sparkling sapphire
sea, and felt an overwhelming sense of peace.

Last time he'd come here he'd brought a simple day pack. Today he had three bags of gear in
the cargo hold. Most of it was medical equipment
which would stay here regardless of today's outcome. Some of it was personal.

Some of it was the baggage of a man who
hoped he was coming home.

Nothing was settled. He should be apprehen-
sive and part of him was, but there was also a
core within him that felt complete.

These last eleven months had been long and
fraught. He'd worked desperately hard to achieve
what he'd be presenting to the islanders today. It
had been an enormous challenge, and there were
challenges yet to come.

But underneath... As the months had worn on,
as the 'friendship' calls to Elsa had grown longer, as he'd had to summon an almost superhu-

man effort to hold his emotions in check during her one visit to Sydney in July… As he'd fought with his desire to drop everything he was working for and go to her, any doubt of how he felt had fallen away.

He loved this woman with all his heart, and he'd do whatever it took to win her. He hoped today that he was providing enough, but if it didn't succeed…

'Then I'll figure some other way to be with her,' he said to himself. 'On her terms. I'll do whatever it takes.'

They were circling now, coming in to land. The landing gear settled into place with a gentle thump. The runway loomed ahead, and then they were down.

He was back on Gannet Island.

And the last barriers to his carefully guarded heart seemed to fall away right there and then. Years of solitude, of isolation, of carefully constructed independence faded to nothing.

His heart was in the hands of one slip of a red-haired doctor.

It had to be right.

He was home.

It was a great Christmas Day—as far as Christmas Days went. There'd been no emergencies, no unexpected illnesses. The hospital was quiet.

Grandpa was looking good. Elsa had planned her Christmas gifts with love and care. The island's cooks had cooked up a storm. The hall was looked great, the decorations superb. It was crowded, full of laughter, friendship and Christmas cheer.

Then why was she so flat?

So sad.

It was Ghosts of Christmas Past, she told herself, and struggled to act happy, even if something inside her felt like lead. She watched Eileen O'Hara unwrap dozens of balls of leftover wool collected from knitters all around the island during the year, squirreled away for just this moment. Eileen's crocheted rugs were legendary but she struggled to afford wool. As her parcel opened she burst into tears and then beamed her happiness. Around her the islanders whooped at her delight and Elsa thought that this was the most important thing in the world. Community.

Not self.

Not Elsa, who still felt as if a gaping hole had been ripped open inside her and would never be filled.

Except by Marc. And that could never happen.

She'd been in contact with him during the year. He'd phoned, often, but only as a friend.

In July, Robert had needed a check-up and Elsa had gone with him to the mainland. To Sydney

Central. They'd stayed for only one night, but Robert had gone to sleep early and Elsa had had dinner with Marc.

She'd felt almost light-headed, jubilant with the all-clear her grandfather's check-up had produced, but totally thrown by the Marc who'd picked her up at their hotel and taken her to a gorgeous restaurant overlooking Sydney Harbour.

It had been a different Marc. This was where he was meant to be, she'd thought. He'd looked a million dollars, a surgeon at the top of his game.

And he was her friend. He was only her friend.

'How's it going, working with Stella?' he'd asked.

'It's so good, Marc,' she'd told him. 'I still don't know how you conjured her up, but we work brilliantly together. Plus she plays chess with Grandpa almost every night and sometimes she even beats him. We're so happy, thanks to you.'

'But you? Are you happy?'

'I have everything I want,' she'd said, a little too firmly. 'A healthy Grandpa. A colleague I adore. A fantastic medical set-up for the island. I can't ask for more. Now, tell me about you. I read one of your research papers in *Cutting-Edge Medical* last month. Wow…'

And that was as personal as she'd got. She'd shaken hands formally at the end of the evening and that was it.

Back to the occasional phone call. Back to being friends.

Back to the rest of her life.

They were almost at the end of their gift list now. There was a bundle of new fishing sinkers for Tom Hammond, a dozen assorted envelopes of different poppy seeds for Chrissie Harding and they'd be done.

And then there was a stir at the doorway. She looked up to see a group of strangers gathered at the glass doors. A mix of maybe twenty people? It included young couples, a few older folk, a smattering of kids. A woman holding a baby.

They were all dressed in Santa hats, even the baby.

This must be the group who'd booked out Bob Cruikshank's cottages, she thought. The cottages had only been three-quarters done when, in September, a team of builders had arrived from the mainland and completed the job in weeks. Bob had been going around looking like the cat that got the cream ever since, but he wouldn't say where the money had come from to bring in the builders, nor would he say who the first occupants would be.

A family group? Who?

It was Maggie who opened the door, but she put her body in the way of anyone entering. 'I'm sorry,' she said, kindly but firmly. 'This is a private function.'

And then there was a stir in the group. It parted and someone from the back made their way through.

A man. Tall, dark, lean. Wearing a Santa hat. Marc.

Elsa had been standing by the Christmas tree, handing presents to Bob Cruikshank, who'd been playing Father Christmas. Bob, the realtor whose thigh had healed beautifully after his argument with the chainsaw, held out his arms in welcome.

'Ho-ho-ho!' he boomed. 'These people are welcome, Maggie. These people are a gift to all the island.'

She couldn't make any sense of what Bob was saying but it didn't seem to matter anyway.

Marc was here.

Maggie stood aside, stunned, and they trooped in, a weird assorted bunch. Robert rose stiffly from his seat, beamed and shook Marc's hand. As if he'd expected him? Then Marc led them up to the front of the hall, leaping lightly up onto the stage to where Elsa stood beside the Christmas tree.

He smiled at her, a huge enveloping smile that made her heart turn over. He took her hands and for a moment she thought he meant to kiss her.

He didn't. His gaze was a kiss all on its own,

but they were in front of a hall full of people. She was totally confused, and maybe he sensed that a kiss would send her right over the edge.

'Happy Christmas, love,' he said gently, and she felt as if she was over the edge already.

But then he released one of her hands and tugged her around so they were both facing the audience. Who'd fallen silent, stunned. Expectant?

Bob Cruikshank was still beaming and so was her grandfather. What the...?

'We have a gift for you all,' Marc said, his words falling into a void of hushed bewilderment. 'And that gift might be us. If you want us.' And then he smiled and motioned to the two gifts left under the tree. 'But we've interrupted. Can Santa give these out first?'

'No!' It was a roar of dissent from the confused guests, but when it finished there were two faces reflecting dismay.

Tom and Chrissie.

'Yes,' Elsa managed, and Tom received his sinkers and Chrissie beamed over her poppies, and then everyone looked at Marc as if he was a genie about to produce...who knew? Nobody knew.

'Can I introduce the new residents of Bob Cruikshank's cottages,' Marc told the gathered audience, and proceeded to do just that.

'This couple are Ellen and Graham Parkes,' he told everyone. 'Ellen's an obstetrician, Graham's a renal physician, and these are their three kids, Hamish, Archie and Kim. Next is Angus Knox, a family doctor, and his little son Noah. Then we have Arthur and Lois Campbell. Lois is a gerontologist, Arthur's a general surgeon. David Wyndham behind them is an orthopaedic surgeon. Next is Cathy Graham, a theatre nurse. Then Nic Scott, a paediatrician...'

A host of supremely qualified medics. Here on holiday?

Apparently not.

'We're here to see if we can make Gannet Island the centre of the best regional health service in the world,' Marc said, and Elsa thought her legs might give way.

'No pressure,' Marc continued, still speaking to the stunned and silent islanders. 'This is a try-it-and-see. Some are here for quick visit, to see if they like it. Some are here on a month's vacation, hoping to talk to you all, plus the residents on the outlying islands. We're all specialists, and all of us would like to back off from our city practices. Our thought is to build up a medical base on Gannet that's second to none and, in doing so, provide a comprehensive medical service to the outer islands.'

She stared. She tried to think of something to say.

She couldn't.

'We have tentative plans—and funds—to build a helicopter pad and purchase a decent chopper,' Marc continued, smiling at her before he turned back to the audience. 'Plus we can afford a decent fast boat, capable of transfers between the islands. We'll need to extend your hospital. That'll need your cooperation—everything will need your cooperation—but our approach to the government for funding has already met with unqualified approval. Your Dr McCrae—Robert—has been assisting us from this end. The government funds your health care, either here or in Sydney. It'll cost the government a whole lot less if every major case doesn't need to be evacuated.'

What…? How…? Her jaw had dropped to her ankles.

'This is impossible,' she breathed, staring from Marc out to the group of newcomers—who were all smiling and laughing—and looking really, really hopeful. 'How can it possibly work?'

'Your grandfather thinks it can work,' Marc told her, and Elsa turned to look at Robert. He was grinning as if all his Christmases had come at once.

'These people might just have consulted me,' he told her happily. 'I am, after all, Gannet Island's senior doctor. I had the first call last February, and we've been working on the plans ever since.'

'Hey, does this mean I won't have to go to Sydney for my hip replacement?' someone at the back of the hall called, and Marc nodded.

'If you can wait a couple of months, mate. It'll take time to get things in place but surgery such as hip replacements will be our bread and butter. Also obstetrics. Mums shouldn't have to fly to Sydney to have their babies. If everyone supports us there'll be far fewer evacuations. But, as I said, there's no pressure. We're all here for a try-it-and-see vacation, with no compulsion to commit on either side.'

There was another moment's silence while everyone in the hall took this on board. And then another.

And finally it was the redoubtable Maggie who broke it. She lifted her amazing crocheted hat off her head and walked forward and stuck it on Marc's head, replacing his Santa hat. And then, as of one accord, there was a rush as every islander tried to put their island caps on the newcomers. The silence was more than broken—the noise in the hall was unbelievable as the incoming medics were welcomed into the celebration with jubilant enthusiasm.

Elsa stood on the stage and stared out at the

melee and thought the ground beneath her was giving way.

Before a hand took hers and drew her away. Out through a side door, out behind the hall. Out to stand underneath the giant eucalypt, with its towering canopy laced with glorious crimson mistletoe.

Out to where she could be thoroughly, ruthlessly kissed.

She was being kissed by a guy in a crocheted elf hat with a tail and a pompom. She was being kissed by someone who'd just offered her the world.

She didn't believe it.

But she didn't struggle. She couldn't. This was Christmas Day, the time of miracles, and why not let herself believe for this short, sweet time? Why not let herself be kissed and kiss back as if miracles truly could happen? As if she had any choice?

And he felt so good. So right.

His elf hat was drooping forward. The pompom had swung round and was hitting her nose.

There was nothing like a drooping pompom to mess with the Christmas spirit, she thought dazedly, deciding—deep into a magnificently prolonged kiss—that sense had to surface soon. But not yet.

Just another few minutes. Minutes of holding

him close, feeling herself surrender to his touch, wanting, aching to believe…

And in the end it was Marc who pulled away, who held her at arm's length and smiled and smiled.

And said, 'You don't believe me, do you?'

'I don't have a clue what's going on,' she managed, and her voice sounded…bruised? She felt bruised…or was it winded? She didn't have a clue. 'Is it…? It has to be some kind of a joke?'

'No joke, my love,' he told her and pulled her in to hug her against him again to kiss the top of her hair. 'I'm hoping to put everything I own and then some into this venture, so it'd better not be a joke.'

She let herself sink against him while she tried to make sense of his words. Finally she tugged away. He tried to catch her hands but she was having none of it. She held her hands up as if to ward him off and he accepted it.

Inside there was the sound of celebration, of shouts of laughter, of welcome. Someone had put the carols back on the sound system. *We wish you a merry Christmas, We wish you a merry Christmas…*

A sudden soft wind sent a shower of mistletoe flowers floating to the ground.

Her head was spinning.

'You know I'm wealthy,' Marc told her.

'Medical specialists are always wealthy,' she managed. 'You gave us two great lift chairs. Plus the incubator. I know that was you.'

'But didn't I tell you my parents were independently wealthy? Very wealthy. I've often thought I ought to do something with the family trust rather than keep it mouldering, ready to pass to the next generation, but indecision has left it in the too hard basket. This Christmas…thinking of the impossibility of black geraniums…and thinking of you… I decided why not?'

'The black geranium isn't doing so well now,' she told him, searching for something solid to hold onto. 'We think it's the sea air… Sandra's had to put it in a hot house and hope for the best.'

'I guess there's a bit of hoping for the best in what I plan to do too,' he told her. 'So many things are yet to be decided. But I put feelers out for medics who weren't focused on income, who put working on an island like this right on top of their list of priorities. Amazingly, one column in the *Gazette* had them coming out of my ears. These medics aren't in it for the money. Yes, we have a restricted patient base, but every one of these people value the lifestyle these islands can offer as much as the medicine they can provide.'

'I still can't believe it,' she stammered.

'Then watch this space,' he told her, and he reached out and cupped her face with his lovely hands. 'This is your own Christmas gift, Elsa. Your generosity to me and to this island has made it possible. Happy Christmas, love.'

She stared up at him, speechless, and his gaze met hers. There was no smile. His look was deep and sure and steady. His gaze said that he meant every word.

'And I have another gift for you,' he told her. 'Or maybe not. Maybe it's a gift on hold.'

Releasing her for a moment, he fished in his pocket, then brought out a tiny box, flicking it open to reveal a ring so exquisite she could only gasp. It was a twisted plait of ancient gold with tiny rubies set into each twist, rounding to one magnificent diamond front and centre. It glittered in the sunlight, a siren song, a temptation so great...

'But not for now,' Marc said softly, and her gaze flew up to his. He was smiling with understanding—and with love? 'I know that, sweetheart. I love you with all my heart and I believe, I hope, that you love me right back. But your deep loves—your island, your grandpa—they need to come first. If I love you—and I do—then I need to respect that.'

'I...' She was struggling to get her voice to work. 'Marc...'

'Yes, love?' The words were a caress all on their own.

'You blackmailed me,' she managed, breathless, trying so hard to get the words out. Trying to force herself to sound sensible. 'Then you… you threatened me. Now you're trying to bribe me?'

'I am,' he conceded and—reluctantly, it seemed—he closed the box. 'But know, my love, that this project doesn't hang on you agreeing to marry me. I won't be taking my bat and ball and going home if you reject me. For me this will be a challenge, and I hope I'm up to it. But Elsa, with all my heart I want you beside me as I work on this.'

'I can't…'

'Hear me out.' He put a finger on her lips and brushed another kiss onto her hair. 'Elsa, when I left last year I wasn't really sure what love was. I was fumbling with emotions I'd never felt before, but if there's one thing the enforced wait of this planning has taught me it's that those emotions are true. Elsa, I love you and want you for ever. No matter what else, that's the bottom line. I want to work on this project, but you take precedence. If these plans succeed then I can see work for me here as a cardiologist, but I'll learn to prescribe sugar pills and cope with teenage acne if I must. I'll even give up medicine and learn to fish if that's what it takes. Because, Elsa, my love is yours and, no matter what you want to do with it, I'll love you for ever.'

'Oh, Marc…' She stared up into his eyes, and what she read there… He was speaking the truth. He loved her.

Her Marc.

She was trying so hard to be sensible—and suddenly she knew what sensible was.

'Then you'd better give me that ring right now,' she managed, her voice a wobbly whisper. She reached for the box and struggled through tears to undo the clasp. 'I love you so much. I know you won't be happy fishing…'

'Hey, I like fish and chips,' he told her, his eyes smiling down into her teary ones. 'That has to be a start.'

'It's a great start,' she managed. 'But Marc, the way I feel about you, the way I've been feeling all this year… The way I've been missing you… Even if this medical scenario turns out to be too good to be true, whatever happens, I know that I want you as my husband for the rest of my life.'

There was a long silence at that. A silence where everything changed. Where everything settled.

Where the pole stars became truly aligned and would stay that way for ever.

'Then I guess that's pretty much perfect,' he said huskily, and somehow the box was unfastened again and the ring was slipped onto her finger. It was a trace too big, but there was all the time in the world for them to set that right. 'So this means that you and me...'

'Us,' she whispered. 'Us.'

'Definitely us,' he agreed—and then there was no space for words for a very long time.

How did Christmas come around so fast?

How could so much be achieved in so little time?

Another twelve months, a score of enthusiastic medics, a government badgered by Marc, whose extended circle knew people who knew people who knew people, islanders who were prepared to throw everything they had to give the island group a medical service second to none... Twelve months had achieved a miracle.

The extension to Gannet Hospital had opened in October but even before that the medics had been working in what had essentially been a field hospital. Most had come for that initial month and simply refused to go home. Bob Cruikshank's holiday cottages had been full to bursting, and there were now a dozen permanent homes either planned or partly built across the island chain.

There were enlarged clinics now too, on the outlying islands. A dedicated boat. Marc's chopper plus a pilot who'd also had paramedic training.

A miracle indeed.

Bob Cruikshank was playing Santa this year at the island's Christmas dinner. He'd pleaded for the job and Elsa had gracefully conceded.

In truth she hadn't felt at all confident she'd be able to carry it off. For the last week her tummy was letting her down at odd intervals.

Hmm.

But she wasn't thinking of her tummy now. She was watching Marc play Santa's helper. He was giving a pair of elbow-length leather gardening gloves to the very elderly Rina Ablett who loved her roses above all else but struggled with thorns against her paper-thin skin.

Rina opened her parcel and beamed, and Marc swept her up into a bear hug before setting her down again and heading back to get the next gift from Santa.

But not before glancing towards Elsa and smiling that smile that warmed her heart, that said no matter how much he was starting to love the islanders, his heart was all hers.

As hers was his. Her Marc. Her husband.

Their wedding had been one special day in November, a ceremony on the bluff overlooking the sea, a celebration that couldn't be held in the island church because every islander and then some had to be present. Every islander had contributed to the celebration in some way. Every islander had been part of it.

It had been a day she'd remember all her life.

Robert had given her away, with pride and with love. Maggie had played matron of honour. Sherlock had been ring-bearer—sort of. He'd been roped pretty firmly to Maggie. There was no way they wanted their ring-bearer scenting a rabbit halfway through the ceremony.

Not that it would have mattered, Elsa thought mistily, fingering the slim band of gold that sat against her gorgeous engagement ring. Not that any of it mattered, the ceremony, the words, the festivities. Not even the glorious honeymoon they'd just spent in St Moritz. She'd felt snow for the first time and it had been magical.

She'd felt married from this day last Christmas when Marc had proposed.

Her Marc.

Home.

'That's the end of them.' The last present distributed, Marc headed back to his seat beside her and kissed her. 'All done. No more presents until next year.'

'There's just one more,' she said serenely.

'Yeah?' They'd exchanged gifts this morning, small, funny things because so much had been given to them this year they could hardly think of anything more they could want.

'I have one more gift for you,' she told him d she took his hand. In private, underneath the loaded table, her hand pressed his downward onto the flat of her belly. Or not quite flat.

His gaze flew to hers, questioning, but as his hand felt what she wanted him to feel she saw his eyes widen with shock.

And then blaze with joy.

'Elsa! Oh, love…'

'Happy Christmas,' she breathed, and it was too much. Surrounded by a sea of islanders and medics, by a Christmas celebration to end all Christmas celebrations, this took it to a new level.

He stood and swept her up into his arms, whirling her around in joy. His was a shout of gladness, of wonder, of the promise of things to come.

And then, as he lowered her so he could kiss her, as he gathered her into his arms, as he held the woman he loved with all his heart, the hall erupted into cheers around them.

They weren't too sure what was happening, but they knew one thing.

Their island doctors were where they belonged.

With each other.

They were home.

* * * * *